Displ:

Derek Turner

© Derek Turner 2015

Derek Turner has asserted his rights under the Copyright, Design and Patents Act, 1988, to be identified as the author of this work.

First published in 2015 by Endeavour Press Ltd.

This edition published in 2018 by Endeavour Media Ltd.

"I'll be great Emperor of the world,
And make a bridge through the moving air"
- Christopher Marlowe, *Dr. Faustus*

For Guy, standing on the edge of things

Table of Contents

I	9
II	13
III	45
IV	53
V	61
VI	69
VII	91
VIII	103

I

Night. Ice. The river scarcely moving, bearing slick reflections of skyscrapers slowly seaward down Deptford Reach. The building. The danger. The delight.

Glass and steel and limestone freeze to his hands as his arms take the strain. Forearms vein with effort as his feet swing briefly clear before anchoring themselves half a metre higher. His face is brilliant with fluorescence from the empty trading floor, and it is full of fierce joy. Not far now, not far – and when he gets there it means another one done. Done and dismissed. He pities those who will soon arrive for work on the wrong side of the window – but only fleetingly, because in this second he needs to focus as if life relied on it. Because it does.

One hand over another again, for what might be the millionth time in his life – one foot finding a niche, and then the other another. His fingers are calloused, yet sensitive, and he sometimes feels as if he is stroking the stone as he spiders up so tirelessly. But a white spider, because his slight frame is clad in close-fitting sports clothes the hue of snow freshly fallen in Greenwich Park – before tourists churn it, or dogs piss it nicotine.

Displacement

The white accentuates the blondness of his fringe and neat beard, although much of his face is hidden by a hood to keep out the cold. Even his feet are white, protected from the frost by highly expensive training shoes that he has had for seven years. He painted over the logos as soon as he bought them to make them his own, and now he would not wear any other footgear for ascents and what comes after.

All this time, his extremities have been feeling and flexing, and now his face is dark as he leaves the trading floor below. He is only two metres from the slightly overhanging steel cornice, and he is briefly puzzled as to purchase. But then his fingertips find a crack others would not have noticed, and it is just deep enough to allow him to trust to it for the second it takes to plant his feet on the projecting lintel. An inhalation, a licking of lips, a hand flung up to catch the cornice, before he swings out mightily by both arms and manages to hook his right leg over. He is safe. Two seconds later, he is swarming onto the roof, and flips to lie flat on his back, looking at the few ineffective stars visible through London's lights. His granddad would have known all their names – a lifetime ago, he had pointed them out as they stood side by side in a field above the Medway. Another one down, defeated.

He stands, so fit he is barely sweating, and his muscles feeling almost no effect from the arduous climb. They had ached in the early days, but now he finds it as easy to go up as to go along. And much better. Down there, he was always done to – up here, no-one is above him, or even on his level. And now for the finest feeling of all.

He walks to the opposite parapet, past air conditioning vents that hum, obsolete aerials, and the remains of a pigeon. He pushes the desiccated corpse out of the way with his foot, gently, not without fellow-feeling. The door that leads down into the building is locked, as they always seem to be. This used to amuse him, because how many burglars would be able to do what he had just done? It had only been much later that it occurred to him that maybe the doors were locked to prevent the people inside from casting themselves off into space.

The next building along is slightly shorter than this – about one-and-a-half metres lower – and separated from it by a gap of around six. He looks down, down into the gap, and smiles faintly. He had guessed it would be good, but this one is better than good. He calculates the run-up required, and decides there is enough. Just. He likes that there is only just enough. The two gaps after this one will be easier, the tops are clear of obstacles. Then the older buildings are joined together all the way down to the junction. Some have chimneys and old-fashioned ironwork, a few sprout buddleia, but there's nothing he can't take. He will be able to get up real rhythm and speed. His eyes expand, his heart pounds but regularly, his mind feels as clear as the unhazed 4am atmosphere, and his feet are perfectly sized and placed. A plane passes over winking, and a couple of cars swish along the Broadway, but they don't interest him. All there is now is the air, and the moment – that perfectly calibrated movement – the concrete roof blurring before his left foot finds the uttermost edge and he leads with his right across the awful crevasse at the bottom of which are sharp metal bins and the cruel street.

II

"Hi, son! All right?" says Dad as he walks in early on Saturday evening. His father is watching *Strictly* in the tiny front room with the frantically busy wallpaper and mantelpiece overladen with ornaments. A family with eleven children once lived in this little house near the Ravensbourne. Martin Hacklett had seen their picture in a special feature in the *South London Press* – the father unsmiling, sideboarded, suited and holding a black hat, the shyly- and tiredly-smiling mother wearing a striped floor-length dress. The thought seemed incredible to Martin, who has always felt the house too small to share even with just two others. It had once been three, but his mother had never taken up as much room as his father and brother. It feels paradoxically more cramped now that she is dead – and his claustrophobia has grown since he started to claim the high places of the city for himself.

He leans his bike against the hall wall, below the photo of Mum and Dad at their wedding – Dad in flares and dead rat 'tache, his hair only slightly shorter than Mum's, both grinning with crooked teeth – and as always places his logo-painted helmet on the bottom newel post. "All right!" he answers, then goes into the kitchen. He ferrets in the fridge and finds a microwaveable health-food. When it is ready, he pours its balanced nutrients and proteins onto a plate and takes it, and a Red Bull, into the front room. He sinks into the squishy chair that corresponds to his Dad's, and his eyes flick without enthusiasm to the screen, where a celebrity presenter with fake tan is being whirled around by a naturally tanned professional.

"Anything going on?" asks his Dad, taking his eyes from the screen for a moment, before they swivel back to the presenter's legs.

"Nah – not really. Busy day yesterday – I was on the go from eight-thirty 'til six. Saw a smash-up in Battersea – some bloke went into a truck."

"Anybody hurt?"

"Yeah, probably."

Wild applause from the screen. An infinitesimal man shrieks and holds up a 9.

Martin looks like his father, or how his father had looked before the fried foods and beer exacted their taxes. He also looks like his older brother Mike – or how Mike had looked before he fucked himself up.

"Where's Mike?"

"He went out with that Yannis an hour ago." His father's voice is full of disapproval. Mike had been with Yannis the night he first got into trouble. This was hardly surprising, because he had known Yannis since primary school. Nevertheless, his father has always blamed the Greek Cypriot a little for Mike's problems – and in this he is partly correct. It had been Yannis who had got first into dope – although only Mike had progressed onto the stronger stuff. And it had also been Yannis who had suggested he and Mike might be able to get in through the back of the mini-market when the Sri Lankan owner had gone home. But it had been Mike, and only Mike, who had made a habit of illicit entries – and it had been Mike, and only Mike, who had eventually gone down to Brixton. And Yannis could hardly be blamed for Mike's involvement with the E.D.L. Another little man holds up a 9. A woman cries.

"What's that?"

"Energy Stew, from the healthfood shop."

"Don't know how you eat that muck!"

"Told you before – it helps me at the gym." His dad has no idea how he really spends many of his evenings.

"If your mum was alive she'd give you decent grub!" Glum silence for a moment. "She used to love *Strictly*. Don't know why, really. It's a bit poncy, if you ask me. But she always liked dancing. We used to go down the Albany Saturdays. She was a good little mover!"

Martin does not like the show. But he does know about fitness, and so looks critically at the action for a few moments, empathizing with the effort of holding those poses even for just a few seconds. It is not unlike what he does, up there where no-one can see, or applaud. He had not known that his mother had enjoyed dancing, but it made sense – she had always been bird-light, right up to the last few days. "Read somewhere that dancers' feet bleed sometimes. Talk about suffering for your art!" he observes through Energy Stew.

"Obviously, it's hard work and all that. But there's no *point* in it, is there?" His father knows about hard work, although he has not had any paid employment since Thames Tides Transport had capsized fifteen years previously. When the little coaster on which he deckhanded had docked for the last time at the tiny wharf in Deptford, long family links to the river had been broken. Those links have almost been forgotten already – although Mike's unused middle name is Doggett, in honour of an ancestor awarded the coat and badge in the 1910s. The little house holds a few fragments of nauticalia – a brass bulkhead clock, a sextant, a red-and-white lifebelt with *Three Sisters M. BN 44* painted around the rim, and a small figurehead of a hippocampus supposedly dredged up on the Goodwins. Martin's mother Fi had disapproved of all this flotsam, saying it was like living in a breaker's yard.

"No point in footie either, is there though, when you think about it?" jokes Martin, who watches the

European and World Cups like everybody else. His Millwall-mad parent smiles.

"More point than the gym anyway, Marty!"

Martin considers yet again whether he should tell his father about free-running. Again he rejects the idea. His dad would see that as poncy too. He wouldn't see the joy of it, the point of it. To him, danger is something to be tolerated, never courted. His feet had trodden decks for decades, but they are planted on the earth.

Martin can see why free-running can be seen as poncy. Because some of it is. This French bloke had written a book about it, which he called "the art of displacement". Pretentious twat. There was a lot of stuff about urban alienation, Icarus and Prometheus, humility, and inner harmonies. Martin still has the book. He has tried to read it, even picked up a few tips from its practical sections – but he has always skipped over all that crap. It is surely enough that it feels good, and is *free*. Doing it is enough in itself, because it allows excellence impossible elsewhere. That no-one else can see him doing it doesn't matter – *he* knows what he can do. That no-one else sees it in a way makes it finer.

He has only once encountered another "practitioner of *parcour*" (which is what the French bloke called free-runners). Doing Whitehall, he had been startled to see an unexpectedly stocky, dark-haired man wearing an orange tracksuit bounding from the opposite direction, like him seemingly at home where no human was supposed to be – like him placing a hand atop obstacles and vaulting sideways, like him circumventing the chimneys and vents and the piles of swollen plywood that so often seem to end up on the flat roofs of old buildings in London. He had known there were others out there, and almost all of them must sometime have come here, to free-run with the grandest backdrop of all, outwit security, jump over the system. But still he had felt irrationally annoyed to have company at a time of private triumph and so must the other, because when he had nodded and called "Alright, mate?" Orange Tracksuit had just scowled before passing on. It seemed there was no community of free-runners, and that seems proper to Martin, who has never known community.

Not even his family had ever quite qualified as a community, because Mum had been so busy, Dad downriver, the telly on, and Mike out (or out of it). Mum's amateur astronomer dad had lived in Strood, too far to see him often, while Dad's dad and mum had died before Martin was born. All the old Omdurman Street neighbours – the Smiths, Masons, Butchers, Hills, Wellers, Spittlehouses, Larsons, Plantagenets, Molloys, Isaacs and Gongfermors – had died out or decamped, gone like Mum's dad to Strood, or Bromley, or Swanley, or Margate. The Hackletts had been the only English in their street for years.

A few other English had arrived recently, but they were students, and their accents and habits were neither London nor even working class. They said "cheers" and "mate" more often than Londoners did, and Martin had even heard one of them tell others "I'm going for a ruby". "Floppy-haired muppets!" Dad had opined, and the evidence was on his side. Whenever Martin encountered these English exotics in the street, they parted to let him through, looking at him when they noticed him at all with a mixture of incomprehension and apprehension, as if he was about to explode. Community was for everyone else. Even at school, others had special strategies, or support groups. The English, he learned without ever quite being told, had no need for interventions, because they had so many advantages as it was.

Martin had started at Sir John Hawkins C. of E. primary with a maths aptitude – where had *that* gone, he would wonder later. As and Bs had slid to Cs and Ds, good behaviour to less good, attendance spasmodic. He had an ear for poetry too, composing his own in secret. But no-one noticed, or was interested if they did. The only things they did notice were that the strikingly pale stripling liked to climb, had an uncanny ability to balance on and run along horrifyingly narrow walls and railings, and was unusually pugnacious in the playground. One teacher nicknamed him The Rodent, and that was how he had ever afterwards been referred to in the staff room. They had not been sorry to see him leave.

Martin had entered Samuel Pepys Comprehensive with low expectations, which was lucky because the staff were busy with training courses, union resolutions, stress-related illness, and turning Sam Pepys into Aspire! Academy. The most useful result of this metamorphosis, from Martin's point of view, was the complete refit of the gym and playing fields, a zone he resorted to the more he became superfluous elsewhere. He loved the gym with its hard realities – the coldness of the climbing bars, the springiness of the parquet, the thunk and recoil of springboards, the burn of rope, the thwack of balls against walls, the smell of polish overlying sweat. He avoided team games, although he was good at them, but beyond the football pitches there were also running tracks, obstacle courses, high and long-jump pits. He frequently stayed long after school, running, climbing, vaulting and catapulting himself over ever higher obstacles and wider gaps until the daylight went, or the caretakers told him where to go. He continued reading and even writing poetry, but his conversation atrophied, because there was never any opportunity to use any of the beautiful words that raced in his head.

Had it not been for P.E. burning off energy and staving off some of the boredom, he might have been like Mike, who had been at the school two years before. Mike had by all accounts been a pest to the teachers – always down the back when he was there at all, hanging with the stupidest and most insolent, chortling and sometimes smoking. Yet Martin remembered him once fixing the engine in their old Ford in minutes flat. And he had been – and still was – an astonishingly good singer. Martin found it unaccountably affecting to hear the beautiful tenor that would occasionally erupt out of Mike's ruined mouth. Even in the middle of the Millwall home crowd his voice was sometimes noticed as he joined in on "Let 'em all ... come down ... to The Den". He could have done something with that, maybe, but drugs and the need to pay for drugs had taken precedence – "skag 'n' swag", as Dad called it disgustedly. Mike used to talk about trying to get onto *Britain's Got Talent*, but never got round to applying. He never would now. His falling so short in everything had made Mum distraught. She had so badly wanted her boys to succeed at something – to be noticed.

It was not only being hyper-fit that had saved Martin. It was also that sometimes he would use his unusual strength and agility in wild and unexpected ways. He had always had what his Dad called, half-admiringly, "a berserk streak". A few years after he started at Aspire!

he had been targeted by the black lads. They had picked off the other white lads one at a time, then the Turkish and Vietnamese – recruiting some to pimp-roll with them, and take their side when necessary against the troublesome Paki Massive. At last swart eyes had lighted on Marty Hacklett, towards the back of most classes except English, solitary, quiet, slight, blinking. He had not heretofore seemed worthy of attention.

One Friday after school, their leader Marcus, abnormally tall and fat and supposedly the son of a Yardie, had gathered his cohort round Martin outside the gates. There were girls there too – hair in Amy Winehouse cuts, arms folded, simultaneously chewing gum and smoking, looking at Martin with appraising eyes as if wondering whether he would make a good-looking corpse.

"Where you going, *Marty*?" Bass.

(Gulp.) "Home, Marcus." Treble.

"We're going that way, aren't we lads?" Sniggers. Yeahs. "We'll go together. Where *do* you live, anyway?" Sniggers. Swaggers. They moved off with him in their midst like a very small prize.

The subway would be the place. It was always there, while the lorries were pounding endlessly overhead – down there among the plastic bottles and glass and sad leaves whirled there from the lone, lopped plane on the traffic island. There joshing would become jostling, and they would push him between them like a ball, laughing. It was down there they would come terrifyingly close, sarkily speak from inches away, ruffle his hair, tug at his collar, pull at his arms, go through and discard his school stuff, take his keys, money and phone. Maybe worse. Maybe much worse. There had been a Scots bloke called George, whom they had stabbed and dumped to die. Luckily, a passing West Indian matron had called paramedics and the law.

Martin knew if they got him down there it would mean at the very least the end of his independence – his pride. And what else did he have if not these? He walked along pinioned by them, deaf to their stunted talk, unaware of the heat of the sun, looking to passing people and cars, and into shops, wondering whether he could break away and get safety somewhere, from someone. But the shop-fronts looked unwelcoming, no-one dared to look at the boisterous group, and then they were at the mouth of the subway.

Desperate valour had boiled suddenly. Dad had been a fighter, still was. He wouldn't allow this to happen to *him*. With that, Martin had rushed to the right, knocking aside two unsuspecting captors, and got his hand on top of the railing. The gods of the gym interceded, granting him the power to leap up and pivot on his wrist. His legs cleared the railing miraculously, and as he swung round on his wrist he got a circular glimpse of shop fronts and startled faces, before his feet lighted gracefully on the ground. He had just time to be grateful for that grace before he cannoned into his tormentors from behind, pushing two face-first down the concrete steps, and then another, in an outburst of manic energy. His captors had still not got past the stage of shouting "Fuck!" or "Watch out!" before Martin had kicked two more between their legs. They folded and fell, their girls screeched and stretched out nailed hands, and Marcus and the others backed away while Martin hailed ferocious kicks into the faces of the fallen. Marcus's remaining lieutenants made as if to pile in, but Marcus shouted "Leave him! He's *mental*!", while admiration grew in his piggy eyes. He gripped two attacking girls by their biceps, and they had to be satisfied with spitting as they saw their boyfriends vanquished.

Then Martin realised what he was doing – became acutely aware of the frantic busyness of the High Street and the main road, the horrified expressions of drivers and passers-by. Curses and moans rose from the ground and the maw of the subway. "Darren's knocked out!" shouted another one who had gone down the steps as he limped back up, and all the protagonists stared at each other for the longest of seconds before they broke and ran in different directions.

Martin, fittest and guiltiest, ran quickest, down through the dreaded subway, clearing dreaming Darren in a bound, threading in a flash through shocked assemblers and up the other side, to lose himself in seconds in back streets known since infancy. He barrelled in a panic past ex-council blocks and the Dockyard entrance with its cattle skulls, through the park with its crutched mulberry, and past St. Nicholas church, with the limestone death's-heads on its gate pillars. *He* was dead tomorrow, he told himself – as dead as that Marlowe bloke in the graveyard. "Cut is the branch that might have grown full straight" – that might be *his* epitaph too!

Martin stopped only when he got to the river, brought up abruptly as always by its stately fullness. Here he loitered fretfully for hours, attracting curious glances from rare strollers, and suspicious ones from the brutal blocks of the Pepys Estate. He replayed the violent encounter over and over with a mixture of satisfaction and apprehension, hopped over cannon and walls to take his thoughts off tomorrow, walked on the slimy strand, skimmed stones and cattle bones at Canary Wharf.

He had gone to school the following day tooled up, a tyre lever heavy and unbalanced inside his blazer. Sure enough, Marcus had been slouching outside, so chunky that even ingoing staff would not meet his look. He straightened when he noticed Martin, and lumbered towards him. Martin glanced round quickly, expecting ambush. But Marcus raised a pudgy hand, and a smile altered his usually ugly face.

"You're fucking *mental*, Marty, you know that? Respect! Never seen one take on eight before!" He chuckled. "You're fit as *fuck*, man! Never seen anything like that! Just wanted to say you're O.K. with me now. Anyone else try to fuck you over, let me know!" He stopped, plainly expecting gratitude, but a nonplussed Martin said nothing. Marcus hesitated, then smiled brilliantly. "Anyway, you're one *proud* motherfucking dude! See you round, Marty!"

Marty had no more trouble from Marcus or his followers, other than scowls from Darren, who came back with stitches. Marcus even invited him to hang with them, and did not seem to mind when Martin lied that he couldn't make it. "O.K. Marty, O.K. So you run alone! Fair dos!" He would sometimes stop to high-five and talk, while the Darrens skulked behind, resenting the favouritism but afraid to cross their leader. He also stepped in to protect Martin at least once, warning off a newly-arrived Syrian syndicate. Maybe he spent too much time talking to these, because a few years after leaving school, and after a second time inside, Martin heard Marcus (now slim, and named Muhammed) had gone off to Syria to fight. Martin knew he should hate him for this – Dad and Mike had been incandescent when they had heard that someone from *their* school had become a traitor – but to Martin this seemed too easy. Marcus was a shit, sure, but he had been failed and fucked over too. Who *hadn't* been?

One unexpected and game-changing outcome of standing up to Marcus was that a girl who had been there had come onto him. *The* girl! Martin's first – his only – real one. Kate Fuller's lightened hair was usually yanked into a cruel Croydon facelift and she was too heavily made-up. Her clothes and musical tastes were bog-standard, and she had been just another Marcus camp-follower, looking on with empty eyes as he barged and beefed through school. But seen up close, and by herself, Martin saw she was pretty. She didn't have any tattoos, and had never pierced her nose. Not only that, but she was unpretentious, intelligent and devoted to her mother, who was suffering early-onset Parkinson's. She admired strength of mind as well as strength of body. His indigo and her emerald eyes locked on and flashed out together, like an expensive engagement ring in a jeweller's window.

They would go steady for two years. Good years. The best. Years in which he learned how to talk to someone who could understand where he was coming from, and reciprocate in kind. Years in which he learned that wanting and needing were sometimes the same thing. They walked by the river to Bermondsey and back again. They went to the urban farm at Rotherhithe, or talked endlessly in Sayes Court Park. He showed her the mulberry, and the fig on the bank of the Ravensbourne, which he knew about because tree-mad Dad had told him. Also other things Dad had told him – ship-building, the Pool thick with masts and funnels, cranes bowing to the *Havengore*, the whale harpooned in Deptford Reach hundreds of years before, the whole semi-secret riverine geography that underlaid the southern shore. She had refused to believe the whale story, or in the existence of Evelyn who had recorded it, because Evelyn was a girl's name. That he could put her right on such things made him feel wise for the first time. That she could put him right on many others didn't bother him. They were on a level, and while apart they texted from early to late.

They dared Nunhead at night when wraiths of moistness were rising from the ground, and she was deliciously terrified as he darted out at her from behind ivy-strangled mausolea. She drank too many alcopops in Rotherhithe, and again in Penge, while he had too much lager. He helped her pack in the fags. They dropped E together and danced to whatever was played, although he liked driving rock while she preferred soul. They watched films about superheroes and she would tease him for saying what some of those characters did really could be done. They would get a train into Charing Cross and wander round town looking in windows, laughing at the crap people bought. He even shamefacedly let her see a few of his poems, feeling better about it when she told him she thought them lovely, and they should be published.

One August afternoon they went to Bromley Common, and processed hand-in-hand by the Ravensbourne, which rose there to flow north through ever-more graffitied neighbourhoods and defiled holy wells to become Deptford Creek, before losing its identity in the Thames. "Funny," he observed, "this little stream becoming that, with its fig-trees, and trolleys. Sad, really!" - and she agreed it was. He knew what was coming down the bourne, and he was full of excited trepidation. He lost his cherry an hour afterwards in a brake of silver birch and bracken, and he didn't care that it wasn't her first time, or even her second or third.

"Marty," she had enquired dreamily, still not dressed, resting on one slim arm, gazing down at him with a new and delightful softness. "What'll you do when you leave?" It was their second-last summer at school – although for all he was achieving he might as well already have left. She looked stunning, he had thought, with her hair down – and he stroked her bare shoulder as he replied. Light stippled her like a fallow deer. Seen from that angle, life had looked long, and hopeful.

"Dunno really. What about you?"

"Dunno either. Never thought about it. Don't really wanna work. Mr. Finn says I should think about the law, or business, or maybe politics. There's nothing I can't do, he said! More women needed everywhere, he said."

Martin had been surprised. During his meeting with the school careers guidance counsellor, the only suggestions had been working for the council, or perhaps the infantry. If they were recruiting at the time. Kate's results were better than his, admittedly, but were they that good? In a way, he hoped not – although he realised how selfish that was. But the idea of her being distanced by success was too disturbing.

"Always wanted to work on the ships. Dad wanted that for Mike and me. Dad's dad used to crew a tug, so there's what you might call a family tradition. Dad always goes on about how good it is down the river – says Essex and Kent start to blend into the sky when you get past Tilbury. All clean and clear. Big dawns, big sunsets – the biggest he ever seen. Birds, seals, dolphins, porpoises, sharks. He used to go over to Rotterdam. Belgium too. Denmark, Germany, Sweden, loads of places."

"Cool! Hard graft, I bet, though. Dangerous too. Dirt. Rain. Cold. Storms. Makes me shiver just thinking about it! Wouldn't pay much, and you gotta think about those things."

"It paid enough for Dad and Mum and me and Mike. But maybe you're right. Think I'd have liked it, though." In that clearing, his eyes had looked briefly leonine. "But there aren't any English ships no more! And I always wanted to travel..." he finished mournfully. The gold flecks in his gaze were dowsed.

She had smiled, and drawn abstract patterns on his sternum with a twig. "Me too! But maybe you still can, Marty. Wait and see!" With her there, he could believe that he really would see a little of the world. But Kate had looked thoughtfully at her shapely hands. "I suppose I could be a nail technician."

"Working in one of them beauty places? You'd do well – be a good advert! Sounds a bit crappy, though."

"Maybe you're right, Marty. I wish I didn't have to work at all, though. I'd just like a nice house somewhere."

"We all got to work, Katie!"

"Your Mum didn't, did she? I mean, she worked, but she worked at home. Like my Mum used to, before Dad died, and she got sick."

"Well, the world don't work that way now! We all got to work if we wanna go on holiday, get a good car, or a nice house. Only bankers and foreigners can do things different. The rest of us got to make the best of the shit we got."

Displacement

A cool breeze seemed to have sprung up, their vegetable bed turned prickly. They rolled apart and dressed slightly furtively, more embarrassed now than when they had been naked. When they were both fully clothed, they caught each other's eyes again, and smiled shyly. He had held aside the branches for her as they left the clearing.

***

That autumn they got to Ibiza. The following year, they managed Magaluf and Kos, saving for each trip from Saturday jobs. They enjoyed these holidays, but for some reason neither could identify, they were never fully satisfying. They didn't much care for the other Brits they would meet, and they couldn't speak to the locals because they didn't have any languages, and Spanish and Greek society, history and culture were almost incomprehensible. At some stage, they seemed always to find themselves just sitting by some pool, eating paella or egg and chips, waiting for something which would never arrive. "There must be more to travel than this," Martin said at last in Kos. "People write *books* about it!"

The July they left school, they went to Prague for a long weekend. It had been her idea, and they had walked around for the first day in a kind of ecstasy, not knowing where to look next. Neither had any knowledge of the city's history, nor even of the country

– it all seemed so foreign, Catholic, European, white – but with such vistas along each alley and around every corner what did that matter? They looked in estate agent windows and calculated how cheap an apartment would be. They were not the only English people doing this. A couple from Manchester seemed to feel the same way about Rusholme as they did about Deptford.

Martin had briefly thought he was starting to get inured to all the beauty, but that feeling was wonderfully dispelled when through an open door in a cobbled evening alley they glimpsed a white and gilt baroque interior and heard an orchestra rendering *Má Vlast* with verve. He had never heard anything like that. He had a lump in his throat for no reason. Kate looked at and into him, and they stood for a few minutes listening until someone shut the door. "That was lovely, Marty ... like looking into Heaven!" Kate had breathed as they wandered on down towards the glinting Vlatava, and he had squeezed her hand, lost for words.

But the following afternoon, a prosperous-looking Czech in a bar had given Kate the eye, and Marty, four Budvars for the worse, had confronted him. Kate had stepped in to head off a subway-style attack, and she had needed to push Martin out of the place, with the help of a couple of other English lads. He had accused her of fancying the Czech, because he was rich. She had accused him of being a dickhead. Part of him knew she was right. But the slightest hint that he might lose her had always been enough to madden him. What else was there in his life? If he had told her that, maybe things would have been O.K. – but the words would not come, and besides there were people around. Their flight back to City Airport was full of still semi-drunk stag and hen partiers who smelled of old beer and new farts, but the only person he noticed was the one sitting unthawed beside him. She did not speak for the whole journey. She got a taxi home from the airport, while he (always conscious of the cost of things) opted unhappily for the D.L.R. He had not called her. She had not called him. He became used to seeing NO NEW MESSAGES on his phone screen.

A few days later, Dad had noticed. "Not out with Kate tonight?" he asked during an ad break from Cup action. Mike was sitting at the table with an empty crisp bag and three Heineken tins, and looked around with interest. Martin flushed.

"We're not going out no more. We had a bit of an argument. When we was in Prague."

"That's a shame, son. I liked her. I liked her a lot."

Martin had too. Martin still did. Mike smirked, because he had fancied Kate, and he quite liked seeing his high-and-mighty younger brother discomfited. Dad looked at Martin penetratingly, his face cratered in the uneven light from the telly, except for the eerily smooth exposed top of his skull. There was a framed, blown-up photograph of the Kent shore at Reculver on the wall and from this angle his head looked like one of the buoys marking the channel. Yet he looked healthier than Mike, and had more of his own teeth. "Not going to get back with her?"

"Dunno. I'd like ... no – don't think so!"

Martin went out of the room more briskly than he usually went out of rooms. His father looked after him. He loved Martin, although he would never have said so. He could not get to the bottom of him, though. He knew and admired his self-discipline, his well-groomed appearance, his pride, his capacity for hard work. But there was deep water there, and he had never known how deep. His son had always been so self-contained, so quiet and blinking, giving the impression that whatever was going on inside it was intensely private.

Then there was that streak that occasionally made itself startlingly known – those times when, like a squall at sea, the lad could unexpectedly and almost viciously lash out, and as quickly revert to calm. He could talk too, when he wanted to, at times coming out with all kinds of unexpected words, bits of poems and such. Martin had always got on best with Fi – which was the main reason Mike had always resented him – and he had become even more distant after she died. Kate had been a good influence – good-looking girl, from a hardworking background. She had made him more normal. He had laughed more, gone to the gym less. And then there had always been the possibility of a little Hacklett. Ah well, he sighed.

***

Some months after Prague, on his way back from the gym a different way, Martin was thrilled to spot Kate. It was the first time he had seen her since the cab containing her stiff silhouette had pulled out into traffic from the City Airport taxi rank. She was at the window table in Camelot Cuticles, poring over the nails of someone notably stubby-handed, her hair bunched up as when he had first known her, her profile tense with make-up and concentration. (So vulnerable and soft, in the Bromley bracken!) She was so intent that she had not noticed him as he passed, even though he slowed down almost to a stop until he was opposite, only a few feet away. But she never looked up, although her client frowned at him. Unnoticed! Or *unacknowledged*? She *must* have seen him, he guessed darkly – she *must* have! He picked up his pace and passed around the corner, angry for having been weak, telling himself he was pleased she had not made law, business, or politics after all, while knowing he did not mean it.

A few weeks later, he went that way against all arguments. He was dismayed to find Camelot Cuticles had closed down, with drifted H.M.R.C. letters and half-pushed-in pizza leaflets inside the glass door. He stood in front of the premises for a moment, then went into the shop next door (the one on the other side had been empty for years). The Bengali man at the till did not put down his mobile, let alone answer in words, but he did find time for a shrug, simultaneously expressing ignorance of and indifference to the fate of Camelot, and to monitor Martin until he had cleared the premises. Martin stood outside the shop, more seriously unsettled than he could ever remember. It was as if some tall building had been silently removed in the night. He stared up at the beetling housing association blocks, fantasizing that she was in one, looking down yearningly like Rapunzel on his ant-like form. He went to the house where she had lived, even though he had been told she had moved – to find that his informant had been correct. The Lithuanian who opened the door smiled charmingly, but she did not know anything about an English girl who used to live here. Perhaps my boyfriend...? But he did not know either, and he surveyed Martin with such deep distrust that Martin could not help resenting it even in the midst of his chagrin. When he shut the door abruptly in Martin's face, at least two kinds of frustration started to his eyes.

***

Martin had been lucky to get his job, cycling across London, delivering packages. Normally they wanted graduates. It was money, it helped with his fitness and it let him see parts of London he might otherwise never have known. The spine of his *A-Z* was soon sundered, as his racing tyres left invisible tracks all across the Square Mile, the W. and W.C. postcodes, and far out into the suburbs. He liked the longest rides best, where there was less traffic, the houses became bigger and there was more green. He wheeled in great circles – Chiswick, Bedford Park, Hampstead, Stanmore, Epping, Chislehurst, Carshalton, Wimbledon, Ham – wondering who lived in such houses, and whether they deserved to. He could never fully imagine himself living in such gardened roads, so far from Omdurman Street in every sense, but he liked to know that they were there, even though the residents probably included the girls who so often cut him dead at reception desks.

In this, he differed from Dad and Mike, both of whom carried heavy class cargoes along with their embattled sense of Englishness. Dad always said he hated the suburbs, that he wouldn't live further out even if he was paid, although he could never explain why. "I'm a Londoner, and this is *home*," he would say obstinately. "It was good enough for my dad, and his dad. And it was good enough for your mum too!" He hated by extension those who lived in the suburbs – "They think people like us are *plebs*!" Then he would trot into the ordered garden to forestall further discussion, to fossick amongst begonias, clip things, shoo cats away, lounge beneath the resin Three Graces, or carry out small and interminable D.I.Y. tasks to the accompaniment of next door's curry scents, and the other next door's arguments.

Martin knew it hadn't actually been good enough for Mum – that in fact she had always disliked the cramped cottage, and disapproved of most of their neighbours. Her grandparents had only been hop-picker, but by God they had lifted themselves up, and never put a foot wrong. She had disapproved of the loose lives of some in their street, and been unsettled by the foreignness of most of the others. She would have liked living in Bromley, or to have followed her father out to Strood. She had even occasionally fantasized aloud about a cottage in the country, somewhere on the High Weald – an old-fashioned, half-timbered house, with an orchard, chickens, goats – and then dismissed the romantic notion with a resigned smile and return to duties.

Bromley would have been far enough for Martin. He sometimes pictured a house that did not have curry smells, or arguments, or a pounding Broadway immediately behind. A big house, with a treed garden, a black BMW sports, a wife (who looked a lot like Katie). Kids. Somewhere near the Common. But he knew the chances of this were slim. Even if Katie had still been in the picture, how could people like them afford a house –

of any kind? They could never hope to get the kind of job that would pay the kind of money needed. This one only belonged to Dad because of Maggie Thatcher – Dad had voted for her once by way of thanks before reverting to Labour with relief, and then giving up on them too. And whatever Dad said, it wasn't much of a house, and Omdurman Street wasn't much of a street. The house could only ever be sold after Dad had gone, and if Mike agreed, and any profit would have to be split 50/50. And why would Mike ever want to sell? He would never get another place, with his record, and without a job. But then, Martin thought, nor could he, even with a job and without a record.

No, he was stuck all right, stuck as much as Dad and Mike until death in Deptford – stuck in this poky house in this noisy street in this shitty city, sharing space with a dopehead brother and his even worse friends singing footie songs and making crap jokes about blacks and Muzzies. Unless he somehow got some great job, or met a rich girl, or his Lottery numbers came up, or someone recognized him for something ... He was stuck all right, as much a fixture as the straggle-haired Irish who clustered around the old anchor on the High Street in hot weather to swig and sing – as the bag lady he had seen lifting bedraggled skirts to piss in the gutter in full view of A2 traffic – as the hatchet-faced traders who every Saturday came once again to clutter the High

Street with stalls selling washing-up liquid, tracksuits and cheap hoovers – as rooted, outdated, taken for granted as the pubs or the pie-and-mash place. He could leave every day to go to work, but like a character in a horror flick he was doomed to return every evening, to find everything unchanged, except that everyone was a day older and more decrepit. Everything and everyone (except the rich and Katie) would keep coming back to the same place to do the same things all over again.

How many times more, he started to despair, would he push his Yale in the door, place his sweat-stained helmet on the newel, walk to the microwave then the TV, grunt similar things to Dad and Mike, push the same bench-presses, and drop a pointless poetry book as he slid into sleeps that were dreamless except for those when he was falling – until one day would come a sleep from which he would not wake? Already his face was as wind-shellacked as a ship's prow – already his hair was starting to recede – his be-shorted legs looked like beef-jerky – and still all the streets he looked down in passing looked like dead ends.

**

At last, out of nowhere had come a weird kind of answer – or if not exactly an answer, at least a welcome distraction from having to seek an answer to such a painful and perplexing question. It had been a certain late-night documentary, which he had been watching out of sheer idleness. It was mid-week, and raining outside, the least propitious possible background for anything. Dad had been half-waking in the fug, faint snores marking the moment when the effort to stay awake proved too great, and then harrumphing every now and again, as if slightly indignant at any suggestion that he had nodded off. But he and Mike became fully alert as the first frames of the programme showed tiny acrobatic figures coming rapidly into view from the left. Swiftly all sleepiness was banished, as they exchanged acerbic or disbelieving comments. "Blimey!" "No *way*!" "Stupid sod!" "Fucking hell!" Mike had needed to apologise for the last, because Dad never allowed swearing in the house, even though Fi was no longer there to glare. Both agreed the jumpers were insane, that this was a wholly pointless exercise, that the Old Bill should stop it .. .and yet, they watched, leaning forward as far as paunches would permit, transfixed despite all their common-sense, entranced against their wills by the arrogance and elegance, part-fearing, part-hoping for a fall.

Martin had been entranced too, but *with* his will. *All* his will, because this new and shining sport could have been *made* for him. He said nothing while it was on, forgetting to eat but drinking in grace instead, wishing the others weren't there to spoil the feeling of seeing his future. He envied the jumpers everything – the gushing girl reporter, their supreme fitness, their insouciant command of the air, and the airwaves. Yet these were not bred to the purpose, but ordinary blokes from shit places – blokes a bit like him, blokes a lot like him, but who had taken their crap chances and created something new and better, outside the rules, beyond the boundaries. They were top of their own table, on top of the world looking down on creation, yet always looking up and keenly along in a world that suddenly had no walls. Through sheer effort and imagination, they had made a space for themselves, engraved their names on a world which would have blanked them.

Blokes like these could be met in any pub, or down the back of any comprehensive class – casually dressed, carelessly spoken, all outwardly the same – yet in a parallel game they bounded walls, burst barriers, let foolish fears flake away, did things hardly anyone could do in places hardly anyone went. Faced with old and impossible rules they were imposing their own. They were defying not only government but even *gravity*, making their own real. He enlisted inwardly at once, although he remained outwardly still – except for his hands clenching as he devoured their declarations of independence from *all* laws. They had not only conquered themselves, he thought – they had captured a city.

III

So he has risen out of the common, climbing out of London's gorge as determinedly as those Yanks who had climbed that cliff in Yosemite. His climbs are much less impressive than theirs, and in any case the climb is mere prelude to the parkour. But he knows their techniques, and uses some – chalked fingers, close-fitting shoes, ways of testing handholds and toeholds before trusting them, ways of shifting weight and mass, ways of breathing, ways of thinking, when to rest and when to go.

He likes old buildings best. They are less challenging than modern blocks, but they have character and texture, and are easier to get at. The blocks are all glass and steel, like a Specsavers window, and they give little back to the touch. It is pleasanter to feel two hundred year old pediments and decorative details with fingertips, cup weather-rounded swags and scrolls as if they were breasts, poke shoes between hand-made bricks, although of course he has to be careful that time has not made the architecture unsafe. There had been a nasty moment on a Victorian turret in Streatham when an acanthus frieze had crumbled as he stepped onto it.

There are also more interesting things to see through the windows of old houses, the ones that haven't been turned into offices. He almost always climbs in the small hours, and especially at winter, but he still gets glimpses into the kinds of lives he will never know. He sees rooms stuffed with antiques and with more books than Deptford's Library, glowing fires, people playing expensive musical instruments, beds with sleepers or shaggers, lonely-looking people at computers, once a girl crying so hard that he longed to knock on her pane, once even a trannie waxing his breasted chest. Of course, occasionally he is seen – a pale night-terror looking eagerly in as yawners look casually out – or dogs hear if they do not see him, and raise a ruckus as he hoists himself past their scratchy sentry-post.

There have been a few narrow escapes – alarms raised, people throwing open windows, or rushing out into the yard. Some call the Old Bill – burglar! all in white! climbing up our wall! looking in at us! gave me the creeps! – although Martin has always long melted away by the time their cars whirl to a halt below. Close squeaks just make the whole thing better, because as well as the physicality there is also now an element of wit – the winding-up and tease, the knowledge that he has left a memory of himself even if only as a ghost. Maybe you can afford a house, he thinks, but you can't do *this*!

When he gets onto their tops, unnoticed or not, he is again in uncharted territory, where no-one else (probably) has been since they were topped out – a planetscape of angles and slopes that need to be negotiated, any one of which may prove too sharp or sloped, any one of which may catapult him outwards and down. Birds and sometimes rats and cats are the only living things he finds, and he can be almost certain he will meet no-one else – especially as he usually opts for odd target areas, suburban streets beneath the notice of more snobbish *traceurs*.

For the thrill, the practice, and the sake of completeness, he has done as much of Whitehall, St. James's, Belgravia, Fitzrovia, Mayfair, Aldgate and the City as he can manage. Some buildings are too sealed off to get at. He would dearly love to do Buckingham Palace, Downing Street and Tower Bridge, although he is not interested in the Gherkin or Shard. *But* ... he has leapt medieval alleys, surmounted merchant banks and ad agencies, careered across the lead roofs of famous churches and livery halls, and met the Monument on equal terms. He has seen predictable places from a totally different vantage point. There have been moments when everything seems to come together, and in his absolute uplift he feels the way he had felt once standing outside an opened door in Prague, bathed in blood-stirring music. Yet these moments are often followed by melancholy – thinking Kate and me walked down there, and he seems to see him and her there even now, small, pathetic, earthbound. Happy.

Having done so much of central London, he has switched his attention outwards, using his courier trips to scope courses, looking up at rooflines as he passes, following terraces with his eyes to see where they terminate or join others, what climbable churches or monuments. What are the opportunities – what likely vistas, what extended runs? What potential problems – gaps too wide, crumbling brick or slimy stone, weak roofs, wires, railings, cameras, alarms, police stations or other 24/7 busy places? Is the quickest way to cycle there and back in the middle of the night? Where should he hide his bike? He sometimes takes photos with his phone for reference, a whip-thin wheeler invisible inside high-vis Lycra, one foot on the kerb, the other poised on the right pedal for a minute before shoving off again into the unforgiving traffic. Other times, he stands in front of reception desks in suburban solicitors' offices while they snatch his cargo, and thinks something like you rude cow, tonight when you're snoring beside your boring husband I'll be mounting your walls!

He selects his areas almost at random – sometimes simply because he has been there recently and they looked interesting. Other times, he has never been to an area and feels he should explore it. Yet other times it is because there is a gap in the large-scale black and white street atlas on which he records the details of his runs in yellow highlighter. Or maybe a particular building or group of buildings draws him. He scales factories, power stations, railway stations, hospitals and cemetery chapels. He looks down onto extensions, conservatories, pools of koi, vegetable patches, building rubble, sheds, yards, graveyards and gulfs where even at noon no light can penetrate.

And every night he goes out he gets back to his bike and pedals home before Dad or Mike are awake and, depending on the day and time, either goes to bed or showers for work. Dad sometimes says he looks tired. Later, he takes out his street atlas from under the bed, and carefully inks in each run, marking the date and sometimes adding timings or laconic marginalia – *Dobermann lose. Girl with violin. Rats on roof. Fox barking on wall. Scrap going on in No. 5. Lezzers at it!!! Best run of 14. Bill with guns – close one!!!* Large parts of London sprout a new acid-yellow aerial geography. He leafs through the ring-bound pages and relives his exploits – sometimes lets it fall open on a virginal spread so that Fate can be his guide.

Bill with guns – close one!!! This had been recent, in Kennington. The house he had jumped belonged to an MP, a government minister who had been the object of Islamist death-threats. Her house was accordingly ringed with sensors, alarms and cameras, and had a panic button to the nearest armed response unit – and Martin had not noticed one of these cameras, a minute but business-like silver rectangle mounted on a chimney that had clicked into action as soon as it had detected movement where none was authorized to be. Usually, it only picked up pigeons, riffling, preening and defecating importantly on the parapet. But now it filmed something new – and at first the policeman monitoring the cameras thought he was dreaming.

A full moon was setting, and in front of it, almost as if it had been born out of the moon, a pale automaton was moving incredibly rapidly, *running* where it was dangerous even to stand, leaping yawning gaps, its every movement full of a terrible efficiency. It came on, robotic, astonishing, eerie, graceful ... on and on – and then it had gone, out of view even more precipitately than it had arrived, making the roof space even deader than it had been, giving just one split-second unfocused glimpse – left shoulder, a hood, a light and jutting beard, perhaps the tip of a nose. He had not been picked up by any other cameras, and the armed Uniform who had raced to the scene at first did not believe anyone could have been up there at all.

The footage was sent to HQ, where it was watched by an alert sergeant who was reminded of other fleeting sequences he had seen – fragments from cameras elsewhere in the capital, including many highly sensitive addresses. He watched them again, put them all together, and notified his superior.

IV

Precious Biafra-Johnson cannot sleep. She has tried Igbo infusions. She has tried Spar Tonic Wine. She has tried reading *The Nation*. She has turned on television, then snapped it off, disgusted by a stand-up's crudity. She resorts to prayer. There is no obvious physical reason for her sleeplessness, so maybe she is being kept awake for some Reason. She tries to think of anything dubious she has done, but fails. She is exasperated. It is a multiple wedding at church the following morning – *this* morning! – and she needs to be in good heart. Her voice rules the right-hand side of the choir. Her vast ebullience (and bulk) helps cram the former Anglican church twice every Sunday, as she and other Mothers sway and clap and sing and weep, and sometimes become overborne, cast to the floor or thrust to the front to testify to forces beyond their control. Sunday is the highpoint of every week, and Precious is one of the highpoints of every Sunday for her co-congregationalists.

She twitches aside the net curtain and looks out, hoping to see something significant. This is, in a way, her duty, as Stargazer to her congregation, speaker of the Spirit voices, drawer of the secret drawings. Snow is falling across Hoxton – silent, slow, steady, slightly unnerving in its patient creep. She has never liked snow – it is the appropriate blanket for this angular country. Nothing is moving out there. Parked cars have an inch-thick cover on their tops and bonnets, and the leafless lollipop trees along each side of the road look like they have been machined out of metal. The Thirties houses across are curtained, although lights are leaching from some – perhaps people are watching that so-called comedian. She feels sorry for them. She has leafleted this street often, hoping for better neighbours, but so far to no effect. She resolves to do it again.

She is about to let the curtain fall back into place when she notices something strange. Something very strange. It is white, and she first thinks it must be a trick of the moon, large and low to the east. She strains her eyes. There seems to be movement where there never is any movement, where there should never be movement, except birds, occasionally roof repairmen or satellite dish installers. But nobody would be working at – her eyes dart to the yellow-numbered digital clock – 03.44. Yet there *is* movement! Man-sized movement. And it is fast, unnaturally fast – and getting faster! Coming closer! She puts a large hand over her generous mouth, and her eyes are almost perfectly circular in astonishment and leaping fear. Fields of white poplin heave as her heart and breath come huger, quicker. Her skin shrinks and sticks up in nodules. Her hair feels like it is straightening itself.

"Lord!" she whispers-moans. But it is not He. Nor is it one of His envoys. It is, she sees as it comes horribly swiftly opposite, a ghost, but not a Holy one, sheathed in ivory though it may be. It looks to her like an ambassador from some eternally frozen realm, a personification of Deepest North, as it comes bounding and springing over impassable obstacles, leaping effortlessly over and between unknowing neighbours, rolling as it lands on lower roofs and those rolls turning faultlessly again into runs. It is goat-like – *Goat of Mendes*-like! – too graceful to be real, too light to be physical. No body, no human could do those things and live – let alone do them with such smoothness and speed, looking neither to right or left. Maybe – oh, Lord! – maybe it does not look because it does not need to, because it is a devil and *has no face*! The thing's head is just a white blob, a seamless head-shaped extension of its trunk. She chokes back a scream, because she does *not* want it to turn its blank gaze towards her. But *thank the Lord* it doesn't turn, and doesn't stop, just leaps on alone out there in the vast and silent night, full of dreadful purpose.

***

Displacement

Charing Cross. Martin is on the up escalator, itching to get past two teenage girls sharing headphones and a weight problem. They don't hear him, they don't see him, and there are other blockers beyond anyway, so he is compelled to fidget and fume. Even at the top, he cannot power ahead because the shuffling traffic from his escalator has intermingled with travellers from the Bakerloo and a gaggle of Japanese trying to stay clustered around a lime-green umbrella toting conductress. But the slower Martin does notice what he otherwise might have missed – a newspaper board bearing the words: MYSTERY OF LONDON LEAPER – 'GHOST' IN THE NIGHT

He's in a *paper*! He's on the front page! And there's a picture too, although he cannot be identified from it, because it is shot from slightly below and from the left, and he is, of course, hooded. He is transiting between close-together tops, a cat-to-cat, when he hangs from a wall by his hands and kicks off powerfully against it, twists in mid-air, and grabs onto a wall behind or to one side. It is a blurry reverse silhouette, him white against black and grey of sky and concrete, so clearly he was moving very quickly when the machine picked him up. He cannot identify the location straightaway, but the caption reads: "A white, wraithlike figure has been reported at night from all over the capital – Hackney, November MORE PHOTOS INSIDE". He remembers the road then, that one facing onto the frost-speared Marshes, and that cat-to-cat, the berserk swing and satisfactory *plap* as his hands caught secure hold on the stinging top.

So that's what it looks like, that's what *I* look like, he thinks, examining critically his shape as so often in gym mirrors, wishing he looked more graceful. But then cat-to-cat is not for grace, but power – for feeling his torso twist, and spinning calculatedly in space, knowing the slightest mistake could mean he drops. He tucks the paper into his bomber-jacket pocket and pushes northwards through crowds until he passes under the sculpted archway and into the graveyard of St. Giles-in-the-Fields, where he is the only living presence. He leans against a Georgian wall in thin sun, and reads and re-reads. A montage shows him, or aspects of him, in a clockwise wheel from Greenwich through Thornton Heath, Richmond, Shepherds Bush, Wembley, Holborn and Forest Gate. He half-smiles as he devours the pictures, reminded of things he never knew he had registered – the silveriness of the Thames from the roof of Greenwich Hospital, deer crossing an ice-diamonded Richmond field, the cats that uncoupled as he swarmed onto their Goldhawk Road love-nest, the scrabbling of his left hand on a loose coping stone forty feet above New Oxford Street. There is even a still from the

Kennington run, because one of the police officers who was on duty that night knows the reporter.

It is a short article, simply written, mostly quotes from annoyed, puzzled or frightened witnesses. Precious Biafra-Johnson (also pictured) is the most frightened, and enjoying her moment – "I know what I saw!" she insists. (The journalist must have been looking doubtful.) "That was obeah if ever I saw obeah!" A woman from Hampstead who does not wish to be identified shudders. "It was terribly disconcerting to see these big blue eyes staring in my second storey window, like a creature from a Gothic novel". A senior police source is unnerved for different reasons – "It is a matter of great concern that an unknown person or persons can access key public buildings with such ease. Next time it could be a terrorist." ("Ease!" grins Martin.) The proprietors of a bank whose HQ he has "violated" say they will be reviewing their security procedures. A safety campaigner reminds readers that it can be dangerous to climb tall structures, and seems to take lugubrious satisfaction in the idea that the Leaper might fall. Then there is a short, show-off kind of editorial entitled "Jumping to conclusions", mostly about some mythical creature called Spring-Heeled Jack and epiphenomena of urban alienation, but also scolding the police for lack of vigilance.

Martin folds the paper and pushes it back into his pocket, and wonders what he should do, or do differently. Should he simply stop, now that they would be watching out for him? He never expected this, which he can now see was stupid of him. Of course he was going to be photographed by CCTV or phonecams. And now he was being looked out for, even in a city this size it was only a matter of time before he was taken. And that would mean a criminal record, which Dad would hate. The Bill didn't like people who wasted their time. They'd like him even less when they found out Mike had been inside.

Still leaning on St. Giles, he mulls over the altered situation. And then his phone pings – a new text. He pulls it out instinctively, although he is not expecting any calls. There were not many people it could be – Dad, Mike, work, a message saying he needs to put more money on his phone and has hundreds more minutes of free text time he will never require. But it is none of these. Instead, it is a message so exciting that he thanks Christ there is a wall behind him, and that the churchyard is so weirdly still – "#LondonLeaper – its U! K"

V

It is the day after the article. Kate looks better than well. Her hair is no longer dyed, and it hangs in a looser arrangement he inwardly approves. Her hand – nails perfect, obviously – cradles the Bacardi Breezer he bought five minutes ago. He nods towards it to break the silence that has dropped down awkwardly between them, noticeable even in the middle of a pub packed to the gunwales with floppy-haired muppets toting lemon-topped bottles. The pub juts out over the Thames, and they are in a window bay looking over at the Isle of Dogs. It is late on a Saturday afternoon, a wet and disconsolate day. A disgruntled gull sails past on a stiffly-flowing, stew-brown ebb. But the day does not look disconsolate to Martin.

"You've slowed down! Remember Rotherhithe?"

She smiles. "And Penge! A few other places too! But *you've* slowed down and all!"

His Fosters is scarcely sipped, but he has a gulp now.

"I need to watch my intake – I can't afford to be heavy – you know, for when I'm up there." He jerks his head at the ceiling, and she automatically looks up too.

Displacement

It had been three-and-a-quarter years since he had seen her in the window of Camelot. Her mother has been dead thirteen months, and Kate has got over the relief, and the guilt about feeling relief. She is still a nail technician, and has been working at a place in Dulwich for two years, where she is manageress – a better class of customer, she tells him, and not too bad a bus journey from the Thornton Heath house she moved into when her mum died. She shares with three women she suspects are snobs. The three of them go out together, and never think to ask her, which she doesn't mind too much, because their talk seems to be mostly of dances and Gloucestershire. The flat is nice though – nicest place she's lived in. She likes Martin's beard, and feigns not to notice his receding hairline.

Martin tries to take her hand and she withdraws it, but not abruptly. He will try again soon. It feels weird not touching her when she is so close. They always touched, held. But if she feels the same she is disguising it well. She looks so poised, he marvels, yet the speed with which she has rattled out her news shows she's nervous. As so often over the intervening three-and-a-quarter years, he wonders how many boyfriends she's had, and hates them all. But he cannot ask her that yet.

"Anyway, Katie, you got to tell me – how did you *know*?"

"Really weird, isn't it? I dunno – really, I don't! Just a gut feeling. There I was, sitting on the Tube not thinking about anything much, and then I just saw the paper. When I saw the picture I just *knew*. Simple as that. I was gobsmacked! I think I must have said your name out loud, because the woman whose paper I was reading turned around and *glared*! I got out at Embankment and got my own. The more I looked at it the more sure I was. Something about your shape, maybe? Or maybe I was thinking of some of the funny things you used to say!"

"*What* funny things?"

"You know what I mean, Marty! All that about society, and all of us being shat on from a great height, and how you wanted to look down on *them* for a change! And then there was the poetry! You was always talking about how much you wanted to *fly* and get away! Used to make me laugh sometimes, you really did!"

"Did I? Did I really say a lot of stuff like that?" He cannot help feeling chagrined. He has never thought of himself as talker, but always as doer. And was she saying he was *boring*? He flushes.

She smiles, all at once at ease with him again – and the gull-coloured sky over the Isle blazes with sunlight personal to him. "Yeah! But you were right, and I didn't mind! I *never* minded, Marty! When I saw that picture, I just said to myself – 'Brilliant!'"

He has her hand again, and she is returning his pressure this time. He doesn't know what to say, but it doesn't matter. Some people nearby look curiously at the intensely absorbed couple, and a highly successful accountant finds herself welling up. Kate is running her fingers over his fingertips.

"I knew they'd feel like that – all rough and dry from the stone. I've got some cream would be good for that."

There are times Kate reminds Martin of his mum, when he truly realises how much he misses female presence in his life, and now he finds himself dangerously uncertain of his voice. He clears his throat, gulps more Fosters, and cannot trust himself to meet her eyes. "Like another?" he nods towards her barely touched glass. She shakes her head, and smiles; she guesses what is going on inside him. Funny, she has often thought, that someone who loves poetry so much can be so bad at expressing his own feelings.

"Have you written any more poems, Marty?"

He has done some writing since he last saw her, but he feels embarrassed to think about them. Some of his recent verse has felt too personal even for him, and he had written with burning cheeks, deleting it almost straight away. The few fragmentary verses he has kept are almost all about her. She cannot see those. Not yet, anyway.

"Yeah – some," he concedes reluctantly, because he cannot lie to her, "but it's shit."

"I bet it's not – I bet it's lovely!" He doesn't really think poetry should be lovely, but high and grand, like a tower on a plain. But he lets it pass. "Let me read some! Or tell me one. Please, Marty!" How can he resist?

"OK, maybe – but not now, not here. Too noisy!"

It is noisy all right, and she looks around with contemptuous amusement. "I wonder what they'd say if they knew who you were!" They smile in complicity. The still watching accountant is sure they are reminiscing about sex; she finishes her gin and goes out into the daylight (which still looks disconsolate to her).

In fact, they are talking parkour. He tells her about the documentary, how enthralling it had seemed, how it seemed to offer physical and mental escape. He speaks of the moves, demonstrating as much as he can while sitting in a very crowded pub, even though it means briefly letting go of her hand – quadripedal warm-ups, feet-first underbar, forward leap, laché, dyno, slide monkey vault, crane jump, 360 tic-tac, and some of the others.

"They say it's not meant to be competitive, Katie, and in a way that's right, coz when you're up there you're alone – but you gotta compete against *yourself*! It scares the *shit* out of me sometimes! But then that's part of what it's about! It wouldn't be the same thing if there was safety nets or mattresses to catch you! It's you up there against yourself, and everything else."

"Yeah, including gravity – and sense!"

He smiles, mostly because she is Katie, but also because she doesn't know any better.

"It's like E, Katie – gets to you, keeps you on your feet and moving! Even when you're shit-scared, even when you're exhausted, it feels like the most exciting thing in the world!"

She feels almost jealous of free-running for a second, as he leans right across the table, his eyes burn and his hair seems to raise itself slightly. His voice is low so the people at the next table can't hear, but it is wonderfully intense. He is so often inarticulate, but he is articulate now, his whole body engaged in the telling as he recounts runs he has done – and, dropping her sense into a stairwell, suddenly she is with him as he charges across capitals.

So transporting is his terminology, and so strong her usually underutilized imaginative powers, that she feels she feels his pain as he scrapes knees, elbows and breaks a cheekbone in his early days. Then she knows his fear as a coping stone comes away, or he almost topples from a rounded railing into a thirty foot deep excavation with jagged iron at the bottom. Perhaps she feels it more than him, because she keeps picturing what he would have looked like if he had not been able to right himself, if he had slid like that stone to shatter on the flags below, or teetered another millisecond on that railing. She keeps replaying images of him twisted and smashed, while he just moves on like a machine to the next obstacle, never looking backwards.

But she also feels vicarious elation as he gets above the lamps and showers in moonlight – sees irregular suburbs set-squared by snow – feels nuclear fission in his thighs and clears ever-larger gaps from standing jumps – gets up astonishing speeds above ordinary streets trudged by ordinary people. It offers, he tells her and she believes, a way to get above things that had once got him down – it reminds him, and now her, of a lifetime of films, about rebels, outlaws, wanderers, prisoners making a break, epic flights. He feels sometimes like Steve McQueen clearing the wire, or Neo in *The Matrix*, accessing an almost unknown world. He can understand, he says, why some might try and read all kinds of ideas into free-running, but excitement's reason enough, and to spare.

As he comes down from his descriptions, he sits back slightly, his fists unclench, he smiles self-consciously, and expression fades from his irises. He is in the crowd again, a man come down from mountains, but seeming to carry with him an aroma of high places, snow and pines or something somehow wafted into South London. She watches, descending from these places herself, fascinated that so much can be contained in one smallish worker for a courier company in a city as unsatisfactory as this one.

"Wish I could be up there with you!" she breathes at last, knowing she never will be.

"I'm glad you're not – I wouldn't be able to concentrate!"

"Would you be worried about me?"

"Yeah, course I would. But that wouldn't be the only way you'd distract me!" Their eyes flash out together for the first time in three-and-a-quarter years. They move closer – they know what's coming down the bourne.

VI

When Seb emerges from New Cross Gate station, he is almost run down by a cheery, beery phalanx of male humanity going west, singing as they go. They are clad in hats and scarves in blue and white, and some are waving nylon flags bearing an image of a rampant lion. "Perfect!" he says to himself, raising his phone to snap them. Two of the men, noticing, give him huge bad-toothed smiles and thumbs-ups, then melt again into the tribe. "Perfect!" he says again, out loud this time, and the word sounds loud in the suddenly empty portico.

There is nobody there to meet him, as had been arranged, and he looks at his watch again to check. But when he looks up again, someone has come as quickly as if she had that moment risen out of the ground – quite a good-looking girl, green-eyed, slender, cheaply dressed. "Are you the bloke from the paper?" she asks, looking him up and down.

"Seb de la Touche!" He extends a hand to shake, which she takes after a momentary hesitation, showing she is unused to the gesture.

"Hi, I'm Kate. It was me what rang you. It's this way." She begins walking east, more briskly than he likes. He has never been to New Cross before (why would he have been?) and wants to savour the gritty atmosphere – literally gritty, because heavy traffic trundles past unremittingly just feet away.

"Who's playing today?"

"It's the *derby* – the Lions at home to the Hammers! Hammer and Tongs, we call it! There's always a row at the derby." It sounds as if she is quietly proud of the fact. As if to prove her accuracy, a police car passes by hurriedly at just that moment, heading in the same direction as the fans. He nods as if he knows about rows. She looks at him, curiously. "Surprised a sports journo don't know about the *derby*!"

He is piqued. "I'm not a *sports* journalist! I'm the Conceptual Arts Correspondent – the paper's first, maybe the media's first." She stares at him. "So the Leaper's your boyfriend?"

"Um-hum."

"Must be kind of strange."

"Kind of." After a moment, she goes on, "But he's totally normal!" She seems conscious of needing to watch what she says to a journalist.

He laughs. "Well, I hope you don't mind me saying that it doesn't seem normal to *me*!" She does not reply. Another police car goes by, as fast as the traffic would permit. "Looks like it's quite a row today!"

"You get used to seeing the Bill round here. They're like a rash."

"Of course!" he replies, as if he knows all about that too. In the right clothes and with better make-up choices, she could be very presentable, he thinks – although then she would lose her authenticity. She knows I'm looking at her, he realises from her half-tolerant, half-contemptuous slight smile. At least she doesn't get offended like the girls in the office. He approves her disparagement of the Old Bill too – just what he would expect, and wants. Such people have historical reasons to distrust authority.

She looks deeply at home here. "Have you always lived around here?" he asks, although he knows the answer. He is mildly disappointed when she replies that she now lives in Thornton Heath. "Is that a real place then? I always thought it was just a legend!" he says, hoping to raise a smile. He fails. "What do you do for work?"

"Nail technician – I'm a *manageress* now." She sounds slightly proud and slightly defiant, as if knowing that it may not sound like much to someone like him.

It doesn't. "So sad to have such low aspirations! Manageress!" he thinks, almost laughing. And your fa- your Dad?" She stops and turns around, slightly magnificent with her hands on her hips.

"Are you here to interview me or Martin?" she demands.

"I'm sorry – it's just that being a journalist we're always asking questions. I was just interested to know what your Dad does for a living. You're obviously an intelligent as well as a good-looking woman, and I'm interested in you."

"Well, Dad worked for Thames Water Board. Drainage Technician, making sure all the shit got to the river, and stayed there!" She grins for the first time. "I sometimes think what I do is like what Dad did – cleaning up after people, making things look pretty, basically making the best of a bad job, if you'll pardon the pun! But he doesn't do very much now."

"Sorry to hear that. Laid off? Downsized? It's a disgrace what the government allows to happen in these disadvantaged communities."

"He's dead! Present employment pushing up daisies at Hither Green Memorial Gardens."

This defeats him, and he turns his attention back to the district. The old Town Hall is a flamboyant essay in Portland stone, with sculptures of sailing ships and nautical-uniformed men, among whom he recognizes Nelson. Some of the houses along the New Cross Road are large and handsome, and he sees similar roads branching off on the far side. He is relieved when they turn left, down among meaner housing. The Leaper narrative would be better set among these drab ferro-concrete-faced houses in their bewildering maze. He is pleased when his guide says "This is it!" and they turn into Omdurman Street, and he sees that both sides are uniformly finished in concrete. "Bit of a dump, innit? Fritz would've liked it, I bet!"

"Fritz?"

"Lang!" She is surprised by his slowness. He is surprised by her knowledge.

No. 31, which is also called Golden Hind House, is older than the others on the street, a Victorian survival judging by its shape, although its original facade has been coated in the same ferroconcrete as all the newer houses. It is notably clean, in fact immaculate, the plastic of the windows and door recently soaped down, the little square of grass regimented and bordered with weedless bark mulch. A concrete midget perpetually wheels a barrow which will shortly be burdened with pansies. Tarnished wind-chimes, a souvenir of a 1975 day trip to Broadstairs, tinkle aggravatingly as he brushes against them. A sign on the door reads "Sod the dog – beware of the owner!"

That dangerous proprietor is there to greet his distinguished guest, Dad Hacklett wearing a clean-on-this-morning cardigan, under which is a black shirt and white tie, to mark the occasion. "Come in, come in!" he cries genially, and pumps Sebastian's hand with a strength that makes the young man inhale. "He's in here! Marty! Marty! Company!" Sebastian notices the wedding photo, the bike in the hall, the courier company helmet, and on the hall table a folded *Daily Mail*. The reading material disappoints but does not surprise him.

Marty rises as Sebastian enters, and flicks off the TV, which has been showing Basil Rathbone as Sherlock Holmes. Leopard-like is the adjective that first springs to Seb's mind, the impression aided by Martin's fair coloration. Then he dismisses this. He is more like some kind of bird, probably a falcon – smallish but well-made, his every movement economical, and his very dark blue eyes slightly protuberant. The eyes glint with perky intelligence rather than mammalian warmth. He shakes Seb's hand, his shake less powerful than his father's, nonetheless suggesting strength and resolution.

"Sit down, sit down! Cuppa?" Dad is in a hospitable flap, and presses tea (BHS china, clever Seb sees) and shop-bought biscuits and cakes on the visitor. The tea is almost black, and stiff with tannin – the biscuits and cake are cloyingly sweet. These provisions stew quietly in their own colours and preservatives as Seb and Martin sit down in the leather chairs, and Dad and Kate take the sofa. When Kate sits down, her skirt rides up slightly and Seb finds it quite difficult to concentrate on his questions. He hopes the Leaper hasn't noticed.

Martin has not noticed, because he is waiting so anxiously for these questions. He now feels more acutely than ever his lack of education, faced with this quick-eyed public-school product who will be expecting all kinds of good sound-bites to use in his article. "Why the fuck did I agree to this?" he thinks to himself yet again, stewing like the tea. But Sebastian, quick-eyed though he is, sees none of this panic – to him, the Leaper is like a wild animal, self-contained, confident in its own strength and prowess, and at home here. He believes he will find in Martin a natural philosopher, simultaneously in touch with his environment and alienated from it.

"So," he begins, "thanks for agreeing to see me. It's a pleasure to meet you. I thought I might start by asking you a bit about yourself – your background, your family, your education, all that kind of thing. Your Wiki and Twitter pages are quite sketchy. I suppose you've only just set them up."

"My what? *I'm* on Twitter? *You* know that?" Martin looks at Kate, who shakes her head. Neither of them had known about the Wikipedia page either. Dad looks baffled.

Seb likes bringing good news about modernity. "Yes, you have 10,000 or so followers on Twitter, or had this morning – probably more now. We've been tweeting about this interview. You've even got your very own trolls! Might be worth you looking at the account, in case someone is taking the piss." Dad frowns.

"Er, Seb, Dad doesn't like swearing, especially not in front of women! Would you mind?"

Seb, who had not even noticed saying "piss", plays along with the old man's absurdly sexist punctilio. "Forgive me!" he asks gravely, and Dad nods graciously. "So tell me first, Martin, how old you are, yeah, and who's in your family. A bit about the family origins. I just need to get an overall feel for your relationship support networks."

Martin manages to enumerate the family members before Dad interjects about long lines of watermen – Henry VIII, Peter the Great, the Doggetts badge – how much his dad had hated the new tower blocks – shame they ever knocked down 'The Light' because the old power station had been such a great employer – sad decline of shipping on the river – Britain, ditto – sad increase in welfare scroungers – Europe – immigration – Fi and her side of the family – what a good dancer and wife and mum she'd been – there's-not-a-day-goes-by-I-don't-miss-her. Seb listens politely to this prolix exposition, his MP3 recorder patient on the formica coffee table. When Dad starts to repeat himself, Seb switches smoothly back to his actual interviewee.

"I didn't get on with school really."

"Why was that, do you think?"

"Dunno really. They just didn't seem interested in me."

"There was one who was!" Kate interjects. "That's where Marty and me met!" she explains to Seb, who now definitely envies him her.

"Schoolday sweethearts, eh? Bit of a cliché, isn't it?"

She flares. "When I first noticed Marty, he had just pushed some blokes down some concrete steps and was kicking two other blokes in the face! Is *that* a cliché?"

Dad, Seb and Martin are equally startled. "What's this, son? I never heard anything about this before!" – "Seriously?" – "Shut it, Katie!"

Kate feels she had made a tactical error. "He had to! They was goin' to *kill* him! There were *eight* of them!"

"Is that right, son?"

"Yeah, Dad, it's true all right. Leastways – I dunno if they were going to *kill* me, but there *were* eight of them and they *were* going to pinch my stuff and kick my head in."

Dad sits back, satisfied. "Well that's different then, ain't it? No court in the *land* would convict you of defending yourself. *Would* they?" he enquires of Sebastian, whom he sees as someone likely to know fine points of law.

"Well I don't really know, Mr. Hacklett, not being a barrister, but it does sound as if Martin would have a very strong case if this were ever to come to court. But I don't think it will ever come to that, do you? Lots of people like Martin could probably tell similar stories about their schooldays." He is delighted – this is the kind of picaresque detail he has longed for.

"There's no-one else like Marty!" enthuses Kate.

"Lucky bastard," thinks Seb, to whom all other girls he knows suddenly seem intolerably shallow. Aloud, he says, "What I mean is people in Martin's socio-economic group – dispossessed urban youth, underprivileged, ignored by the Establishment, needing to make their own way in a hard world."

"You got that right!" says Dad with feeling. "And what are Labour doing about it, I'd like to know? I used to be in the RMT – you might want to mention that. I read an article the other day says..."

"Dad!" interrupts Martin. "I don't think he wants to hear about all that. *Do* you?"

"Well, I can't spend all day here unfortunately," Seb smiles, "so maybe we ought to try and keep it all a bit more focused. You say, Martin, that you didn't get on with school. Did you manage to get any qualifications?"

"Nah – but I'm not stupid, you know! It's just that – like, no-one seemed bothered. I didn't have no chance, really!"

"He didn't neither!" Kate agrees, loyally.

Seb nods understanding, and asks the schools' names, and about further education provision in the borough.

He is about to pass onto another subject, when Dad says, "Tell him about the *pomes*!"

Martin crimsons. "Oh, he won't want to know about *them*!" But Dad has already stood up and taken a book off the shelf to pass to Seb. It is one of only two books in the room, the other a bulky old hardback. This one is a chunky and clearly much-resorted-to paperback, and Seb would never have expected to find it in a house with so large a TV and such busy wallpaper – *Modern English Verse*. "Didn't expect to find that here, did you? Marty's *mad* about pomes! Always was! He writes them and all!" beams Dad.

Seb flicks through the book – Dickinson, Hardy, Owen, Yeats, Auden, and loads he has never heard of. He knows almost nothing about poetry, and for the first time feels he needs to be on the intellectual alert. The natural philosopher may have unnatural back-up. "This is *great*!" he enthuses. "Some of my favourites in here. But what matters is which are *your* favourites?" Martin sits slightly forward, extremely self-conscious, but also clearly engaged for the first time since the interview began.

"I like loads of them! It depends sometimes on me mood. Sometimes, I like the simplicity of Hardy, other times the richly metaphorical cosmos of Yeats. 'The falcon cannot hear the falconer' – that's a *magic* line! And sometimes I like a bit of Eliot, although to be honest I find it difficult to relate to his eschatological quest. And some of his stuff's a bit gay."

The other three are metaphorically open-mouthed, Kate in proprietorial pride, his father and the journalist in surprise. Martin, warming slightly, is about to continue when a key scrapes in the front door and Mike thrusts himself through with a raucous burst of song.

"Let 'em come, let 'em come, let 'em come,

Let 'em all come down to The Den,

We'll only have to beat 'em again,

Cos we're the best team in London, no,

The best team of all...

Hello, mate! Who are you?!"

The last line is spoken, directed jovially at Seb, whose eyes are fixed slightly uneasily on Mike's St. George's flag shirt. The white field of the shirt is slightly grey, and distended by flesh, but the crimson of the cross blazes out as briefly brilliant as Mike's tenor. Mike has clearly been in the Carpenter's Arms. Dad is not pleased to see him.

"I thought you was at the match!"

Mike hiccups faintly. "They've postponed it 'til they clear the Lane – bit of bother with the Hammers lads."

"Nothing to do with our lot, I'm *sure*!" Kate says sarcastically.

Mike fixes her with a slightly unfocused smile. "Course not!" He turns back to Seb. "Anyway, isn't anyone going to introduce us?"

"This is Seb – he's a journalist," says Martin, reluctantly. "This is me brother, Mike."

"Ooh, a *journalist*? Come to meet my looney bro, and see how the other half live? I hope they're looking after you, Your Lordship!"

"Good to meet you, Mike," answers Seb, although he is clearly uncertain about that. He shakes hands with him, and for the third time in an afternoon is impressed by the strength of a grip. "I didn't know Martin had a brother."

"Oh, I'm the black sheep of the family, me – like the mad uncle locked away in the attic! They don't like to talk about me, do you?" He grins around at them all fiercely, and Seb blenches at the blast of beer. "You see, Seb, it's like this – I been *inside*! I got *form*! And that makes them ashamed – *ashamed* of their own flesh and blood!"

Dad takes Mike by the arm angrily, and tries to lead him out of the room. Mike won't go straight away, but stares at Seb with small eyes, then points at Martin. "Don't be fooled by him, mister. He knows nothing about anything! And what's the fucking point of jumping over buildings anyway – when you can always get in round the back?" He exits laughing at his wit, and

Displacement

Seb smiles uncertainly at Martin. Martin is expressionless, but Kate is fuming. Dad's raised voice can be heard in the kitchen, although not what he says. Mike, Seb thinks, is the bad side of the working class – the angry side, the scapegoating side.

"Err, ha ha, is he always like that?"

"Yeah, mostly. It's just his banter!"

Banter! So people really live like this, Seb thinks – with a dangerous lunatic just wandering around inside their houses, like a World War Two incendiary with a decaying fuse. "Mike said he'd been inside – can I ask what for?"

"No."

"Oh ... O.K.!", Seb says. He can find out when he gets back to the office, because Hacklett is such an unusual name. "Does Mike work?" Martin shakes his head, while Kate gives a sarcastic little laugh. Sensing Martin clamming up, Seb drops the subject. Dad comes back in, with Mike in tow – the latter as sheepish-looking as it is possible to look whilst carrying a six-pack of lager.

"Sorry, mate," Mike says. "I was only taking the pi... taking the mickey! It takes guts to do what he does. Fair play to him! Fair play to you, Marty!" He lifts a can in semi-serious salute to his younger brother, who does not look displeased. "Which paper did you say you're from, mate?" Seb tells him. "Oh," replies Mike. "Don't see that one. Don't read any of them much! Anyway, go on!

Don't mind me! I won't say a word." He is silent for just a few seconds before he can be heard humming a song under his breath. Dad glares, and he subsides.

"You were talking about poetry, Martin," Seb prompts, after a wary look at Mike. "One you probably know is that one that goes something like I have slipped the surly bonds of earth – how does it go? – something about touching the face of God."

"Oh, yeah, Magee. It's all right – bit twee, though, precious in his phraseology, predictable in his metre and sentiment."

"Don't know that one, Marty. Touching the face of God? Fi's gramps wouldn't have liked that! He'd have said it was blasphemy or something!" interrupts Dad. He fetches the other book from the shelf to show Seb. The spine reads *Holy Bible*, in gold copperplate. The volume looks Victorian, an impression confirmed by the foxed flyleaf on which is written the names of three or four previous owners in fading ink. The most recent reads "Edward R. Boswell, Blenheim Street, S.E., 3/IX/1899". "My missus's gramps – he was a Methody parson. Used to go round the camps preaching – lot of good it did him, because he went under a tram in Peckham Rye!" He smiles, as if marvelling at far-off foolishness, but replaces the book respectfully.

"Camps?"

"Hop-pickers' camps – where they bivvied while they was working. Fi's grandparents were hop-pickers as well as being Methodys. But they always liked a song, Fi said! Not just hymns, but old music-hall numbers – Lloyd, Lauder, Jolson, Sylvester, Al Bowlly. They was always singing! Fi was always singing too, some of the same songs! Mike sings sometimes, but not much now!"

Seb has a slight headache, but tries manfully to pursue the poetry angle. In this he is thwarted yet again, first by Martin's father who says, "That If's a good poem! Do you know that one?", then by a sudden blast of very loud Bollywood music from next door. Dad looks sharply at Mike. "Mike?"

His eldest son nods "I'll sort it!", and a moment later can be seen stomping purposefully down the garden path. Seb is worried about what might be about to happen. The combination of Asians plus Anglo-Saxon yob seems deeply ominous.

"It's the Rais – they're from the Punjab. Me Dad used to say Frank Drake went round the world from Deptford and now all the world's come here instead!" Dad explains.

"Oh?" Seb replies absently, listening hard. Bollywood stops mid-wail. It seems deathly still in there, and Mike does not return. Seb thinks vaguely of phoning the police, but then feels he must be imagining it, and should probably press ahead with the interview.

"So, um, Martin, when did you first come across *l'art du déplacement*?"

"What? Oh, yeah, right. Well, it was like this. As it happens, Dad and Mike was there. There was a telly programme – Channel 4, I think. We all saw it. Suddenly, there were all these blokes doing these *amazing* things right on the top of buildings – running, jumping, somersaulting, backwards flips – and I just thought *Wow!*"

"I remember it, son!"

"What was it, exactly, about the sport that appealed to you?"

"Freedom, I s'pose. Danger too! The idea of getting high above all the shit – sorry, Dad! – all the *crap*. And I could do it by meself. I needed discipline, but I didn't need no equipment, or training. I'd always been good at balancing and climbing."

"That's right! Used to give your Mum heart attacks, walking along the back fence!" interrupts Dad fondly.

"I was called Rodent at school, because I was good at climbing. Quite liked the name, really – rats is quick and cunning little sods."

"Little sods!" echoes Dad. It is unclear whether he is referring to rats or schoolchildren. "I'm learning a lot about your schooldays today, son! Dunno if I like it much!" But he is smiling. Seb wishes he would go away, but then these families are always close-knit. It is, he knows, an evolutionary survival mechanism in a transgressive sociosystem.

"You say you liked to get above things – what do you mean? What things, exactly?"

"O, you know – all the *rubbish*. School. Work. Being skint. Some people. Politics. Society. Up there all troubles look real small. And you can look up too, and that's a good feeling. As old Oscar said, we are all in the gutter, but some of us is looking at the stars!"

"No doubt free-running gives you a sense of perspective as well as a sense of the poetics of space – have you read Bachelard? You must discern an essential unity in humankind from up there."

Martin considers this carefully. "S'pose so," he replies dubiously.

***

Half an hour elapses with almost no interruptions from Dad, who sits there peering into his son's hitherto hidden depths. Seb does most of the talking, pleasantly conscious that Kate is listening closely to every word. Martin shows them his atlas of runs done, and Kate's eyes are big with wonder. Then a key scrapes in the front door again. Seb goes on edge, but Mike is going straight back out, as the delayed match will kick off soon. He coils a blue-and-white scarf around his bull-terrier neck and pulls a bobble hat in the same shades down over his Cro-Magnon brow, before looking round the door of the living room and bellowing "Cheers, mate!" at Seb, and "Later!" to the others, who grunt acknowledgement. Seb is relieved to see that Mike bears no signs of recent struggle. He fervently hopes the neighbours are OK. The door crumps to plastically.

"This is probably a silly question," he says carefully, "but do you have any idea what Mike must have said – or done – to your neighbours just now? I mean, it's gone very quiet in there!"

"He asked them to turn it off!" replies Martin, looking at Seb as if he was an imbecile. "What do you *think* he said?"

"I did say it was probably a silly question. It's just that – well, Mike is very big – and his shirt ... I thought..."

"His *shirt*!? What's wrong with his *shirt*, for crying out loud?" asks Dad, suspecting oblique insult. He suddenly looks very like his eldest son, and even Martin briefly metamorphoses into his sibling.

"I'm sorry – it's nothing. A silly thought. Just forget it, please."

Kate speaks now. "You thought he was going in there to *beat them up*!" And she bursts out laughing. But neither Martin nor his father find it funny.

"Is that right?" asks Dad Hacklett. "Is *that* what you thought?" He is really angry, and Seb shrinks, fearing condign tribal punishment.

"It's OK, Dad – he wasn't to know! Mike does come over bad. But I think maybe it's time you went."

"Yes, I've taken up too much of your time as it is. Just one more thing – I need a photo to go with the article. I can take it with this." He holds up his phone. "I need a few I can choose from – Martin by himself, then a few with one or both of you. It's a shame Mike isn't here!" he adds mendaciously. Although he is a good photographer, and the camera is high spec, the pictures are not wholly successful. He eventually has to settle for one which shows Martin looking off to one side as if for assistance, and his father beside him, pudgy and fixing the lens with no great favour. Only Kate grins at future cultural historians.

She walks him part of the way back, because the estate is confusing, it is getting dark, and muggings are frequent. "But that means you'll have to walk back alone from where you drop me off!" he says with a gallantry dredged up from some previously-untapped source. "I can't accept that!"

She looks at him amusedly. "To be honest, I don't think you'd be much help if we met one of the gangs! I'll take my chances!" He demurs, but knows she is right. Besides, the idea of trying to navigate this labyrinth alone, with frost spangling the mean grass and dog shit and uneasiness everywhere, is not appealing.

He probably won't see her again, and the idea is curiously desolating.

"What *did* Mike say to the neighbours?"

"You're a bit obsessed, aren't you? He asked them to turn it down, like Marty says. They'd listen to him – they *always* do."

"I probably would too, to be honest! He's a big bloke!"

"Not because they're *frightened* of him, you muppet – because they *like* him! They'd do *anything* for Mike!"

"But *why*?"

She stops and looks burningly at him. "Wouldn't *you* do anything for someone who'd saved your baby daughter from a fire?" She is pleased by his amazement, and walks on. "Mike's an arse," she adds over her shoulder, "but he's not a *total* arse!"

He digests this, with difficulty. He feels guilty for his underestimation. And not just of Mike. He can see now that her face is pre-Raphaelite pale, and internally illuminated. Her arms should be full of lilies, he thinks surreally, her sweatshirt and leggings a grass-green gown. And what was she doing in such a *terrible* place? They emerge onto the main road, the rumble of which has been growing rapidly, and stand for a few seconds upon its multi-hued and merciless flank. He feels like he is shivering awake from some old, long, unhappy story. He turns to her to warm himself, to ask or say something more – but she has gone, and if she had said goodbye it had been taken up in the traffic. He stares back down her side-street for a moment before filtering back into the mainstream.

VII

"They are the despised."

"What?" asks Dad, as Kate reads it out. Martin and Mike have sat up in surprise.

She reads it again, and this time keeps going. "They are the despised – the last minority it's cool to hate. They are spivs, chavs, underclass – they are welfare scroungers, hooligans and yobs. They are the Cockneys, the old English – the first victims of the Establishment, and still in its clutches, unliberated in a liberated world, regressing in a progressive world. They were the bargees, builders, butchers, carpenters, costermongers, dyers, flushers, fishmongers, hop-pickers, labourers, nightmen, stainers, tanners and troopers on whose backs was raised the edifice of Empire. Now, they languish in despair in inner-city islands, without aspiration, culture or education, more Mr. Kipling Cakes than Rudyard, less Generation X than the Generation Without An Alphabet."

"What the fuck!?!" exclaims Dad, reverting to shipboard habit and for once swearing in the front room. "What the fuck!?!" he expostulates again, and his sentiments are echoed internally by the others.

"I'm just reading what it says! I *told* you he was a smarmy git!" Kate's indignation is all the more acute because the interview had been her idea.

She is being unjust. Seb had really wanted to write something better, but there are many demands on his time, and he is surrounded by alternative narratives. He is also ideologically committed and has a weakness for showy prose; the article title, "The Bearable Lightness of Being", had been his choice.

That London into which he had been parachuted for an afternoon had begun to haze out as soon as he got back to the New Cross Road and been shaken awake by the sight of juggernauts pounding down to the coast. The dream had fallen away by degrees as he went West Endwards on the train, and by the time he had been disgorged at Charing Cross all he could really remember was Kate's face and legs, and a few other disjointed images – Mike's shirt, the wallpaper, the aggrievedness of the old man, Martin's surprising poetic intelligence, undrinkable tea and inedible cakes. Omdurman Street had felt highly-textured while he was there, but it all started to seem very insubstantial as soon as he switched on his Mac.

He had badly wanted to set the Leaper's condition in its full socioeconomic and metapolitical context. That was also what the editor expected. But he only had three pages, and these had to include several photos – the one he had taken, and a montage of action shots culled from other sources. Even staring at his own photos of Martin, his father, and Kate does not make them feel real again. They look awkward in front of the lens, ill-equipped, outdated, as if they had been photographed decades rather than hours ago. He stares and stares, wishing he could see them in some other way. He is *so* sorry for them! But he suspects that try as he might to read some kind of future into their faces, this feature will be an elegy.

He writes anyway, conscious more of the need to be aware than to be accurate, at times carrying himself away. He finds statistics on crime, deprivation, drugs, educational attainment by ethnic category, family breakdown, healthcare, political disengagement and welfare cuts. He quotes a cultural commentator at a provincial university, and makes comparisons with other Western working classes. Finally, after seven paragraphs during which his eventual Omdurman Street readers (among his few readers in the S.E.8 postal district) will find themselves alternately annoyed and perplexed, he gets to Martin.

"But one young trendsetter," he enthuses, "has tried to raise himself up from this slough of despond. Literally. And not just to raise himself up, but to soar above it, bursting into national attention as The London Leaper, like David Copperfield 'a reproachful ghost' forcing himself onto our consciences. Several times a month for two years, Martin Hacklett, 24, by day a cut-up courier, has been leading a secret second life. He leaves his humble ex-local authority home in a run-down street at nights to scale and then to soar above some of London's most iconic buildings. It is a beautiful and dangerous protest, full of unconscious art, a ballet of the upper air, a two-finger salute to the bankers and billionaires who own what should be his. His is a Bachelardian poetry of space, a poetry of motion – a poetry not lost on its author, who reads Yeats and Eliot, and writes his own verse inspired by the high places he has climbed to from the very lowest. He is like Yeats' falcon who does not hear the falconer – but it is because he *chooses* not to. If he is leper, he is also Leaper. As Kierkegaard might have said..."

His editor is delighted, and the article has been widely circulated, envied and praised. But Seb is acutely aware that it is inadequate. He tries to ring Kate. Hopefully, she will understand his constraints. She certainly understands the need for the marginalized to engage with radical media, and besides, he feels he had got on rather well with her.

But she isn't answering, and her phone has been left in Thornton Heath. She and Martin are walking slowly by the Shipwrights House in Deptford, talking about the article and keeping out of the way of Martin's dad, who is still fulminating bootlessly about legal action. They had at first thought that the people they encountered must recognize them from the paper, but gradually relaxed when no-one did. Martin refrains from his habitual hopping between cannon, walls and bollards partly to avoid attracting attention, but mostly because at the moment he prefers to clutch her perfect left hand in his stone-rubbed right.

"It weren't your fault, Katie!" he assures her again. "And Dad'll get over it. He doesn't blame *you*! At any rate we got a few quid out of it, didn't we? We could go on holiday. Back to Prague, maybe."

"How *dare* he?" she demands again of the air. Finally, Martin folds her into himself against the cold, and tells her to shut it, it didn't matter, Dad would forget it, and the journalist wasn't a bad bloke so far as he could see, just a muppet like all the others. Eventually, she buries her head into his neck, and murmurs, "At least he said you're beautiful!" Then she shuts it.

It is later, dwindling daylight, and they have almost forgotten the article. Piles for high-end flats are being pounded in at the former wharf, and they pause to look at the artist's impression of the development. Men and women in suits stride purposefully between expensively nondescript towers. A small child frisks with a small dog among flowers. Pure-sailed yachts tack up an atypically aquamarine Reach. The weather of the future is guaranteed glorious.

"Like to live in there?" she asks, jocularly. He points to the "Prices from..." phrase at the bottom, and even she blinks.

"Don't think so – do you?" he asks ironically. "Anyway I fancy a change – I've got my eye on a penthouse in Knightsbridge!" They walk away, entwined, thinking about the same thing. Streetlights buzz on as the evening clusters into ice.

"You could squat on the roof, Marty – climb up the outside every evening and back down every morning! Nobody'd know! But, seriously, what *will* you do? About a place to live? In the long term."

"Dunno. No way I can ever afford to buy a place. But somehow I don't see myself living with Mike after Dad's gone!"

She almost says something, then stops. She tries again, and this time keeps going.

"Have you ever thought of *sharing* with someone?"

"Yeah, Katie, I *have* thought about it! I've thought about it a *lot*! As it happens, I was thinking about it just now..."

"Was you?"

"Yeah..."

They stand beneath that streetlamp for at least ten minutes.

***

Kate answers later, just as Seb realises it is almost ten o'clock.

"Is that Kate?"

"Yeah, who's this?" She sounds sleepy, and he likes that.

"It's Seb! Just calling to check you were all happy – you know, about the article."

"Oh, yeah, hi. The article, yeah. Well..."

"I *knew* it! I knew it didn't do you justice – I mean that it didn't do *Martin* justice. But I only had very limited space. You *know* how it works!"

"Well, no I don't know how it works, actually! None of us liked it, to be honest. Marty took it the best. He even said some of it was funny. But his dad went *mental*!"

"Seriously? About what? I thought he came across very well. That was one of the bits I liked most!"

"So you thought it was OK to talk about his low-class family – to say he was trapped in a time-warp, a – what was it? – yeah, here it is – a life-long victim soured by disappointment, that he used to work on a *barge*, and that he lived in a crap house in a shit street?"

"I didn't say *that*! I didn't say anything *like* that! And I *had* to talk about his family! That's what I was there for! And anyway what did Martin mean about it being funny?" The suggestion that some of his deeply earnest analysis had been found *amusing* really stings him.

"Read it again, and this time as though you was a proud man who's worked hard for what he's got. It may not look like much to you, and maybe it ain't, but what he's got he likes. Read it as though you're not educated. Read it like you're one of 'the despised'! Read it any way you like! I'm not saying it's all wrong – a lot of what you say is right – but ... it's like as though ..."

He comes to her rescue. "... it fails to convey the harsh reality of life on breadline Britain? Or, maybe, whilst sympathetic, it appears to lack real empathy with its subject? Or, perhaps, are you trying to say ..."

"There you go – off again! All I'm saying is that it don't read right. If Marty wasn't such a great bloke he'd have gone up to town to deck you. He thinks the *world* of his Dad!"

"Well so did I! He's a great bloke!"

"Well, doesn't sound like it!"

"Hey, what can I say? I'm *sorry*! But what did you mean about Marty finding it *funny*? There was nothing *funny* in there."

"He was pissed off to begin with, but then he saw the funny side. Wait a sec ... yeah, here's a bit – 'a socialist Spring-Heeled Jack beating on all our doors, breathing fire of social outrage'. Another one – 'a proletarian Prometheus, leaping to shake off the trammels of the banksters, the oligarchs, austerity cuts, folk memories of the outmoded Empire and outgoing nation'. Or 'from his concrete eyrie he can discern the essential unity of humanity. Like angels of myth, he is a winged symbol of retribution'. I mean, for *fuck's* sake!"

"But all of that's true! OK, maybe the phraseology fell short here and there – all writers feel that way about their work, although I have to say my editor thinks it the best thing I've done, and the Twittersphere has been going wild! But the truth of the matter is that although Marty may not know it, he *is* in flight from all these things, and he *has* become an aerial avatar, a symbol of hope to millions. He's a victim, like all of us are, and the sooner he recognizes that the sooner we can make progress! I want to *help* people, Katie! I want to help *all* the Martins!"

"I think maybe you've done enough!"

"Maybe we could meet again and discuss the wider context. I'm sure Martin would see it my way if I could have a talk with him! I've got some interesting news for him anyway. Or maybe, if he isn't available, you and I could meet and talk about it, maybe over dinner ..."

She laughs slightly. "Wait a sec – if you're going to start making appointments it would make sense to speak to him direct. Here!"

"Hello, mate!" comes Martin's quiet voice. Seb flushes. Martin has heard the whole thing on speakerphone, probably while he and Kate had been lying naked in bed. They are playing him along, laughing at him a little – once again he has been wrongfooted by these people he so wants to help, and who so badly need his help if only they could see things clear. Try as he might to enter their world, they are still locking him out.

"Oh, *hi*, Martin! Have you been listening to what we've been talking about then?"

"Every word of it mate, and I agree with everything what Katie said. But there's one thing I wanna add off my own bat – I don't like you hitting on *my* girl! OK?"

"But I wasn't – I mean I only called Kate because I don't have your number – I mean, OK!" Seb has an uncomfortable vision of people being pushed down concrete stairs and kicked frenziedly in the face. He is glad he has some news which should placate. "Look, I'm sorry you didn't like some of the article. I'm *really* sorry if your dad was offended! But the point is that a lot of people did like the article! I mean, they *really* liked it. I don't know if you've seen some of the Twitter comments ...?" He pauses, but it seems Martin has not. Probably just as well, because there have been a lot of negative Tweets too, about the irresponsibility of his actions, the importance of respecting private property, how the old and vulnerable might be frightened, how some people think they own the city, how certain white males have an innate sense of their own superiority and entitlement, and a few even saying they hoped he'd fall.

"Anyway, the thing is I had a call today from a mate of mine who runs a small publishers, and he's *interested* in you! He's looking for someone left-field to write an introduction for a modern poetry collection he's publishing, for a start. It's called *Outsider Iambics*. But he also said he'd like to see some of *your* poems, because he might publish some of them. It wouldn't mean much money – there's no money in poetry, as you know – but it might lead onto other things. He has a great reputation in the field, and this could be a kind of springboard."

Martin comes back on the line, and there is genuine excitement in his voice. Kate can just be heard in the background, breathing-saying "Wow!" Seb pictures her sitting up excitedly in bed, perhaps with the bedding falling away .. .and his elegantly understated flat feels awfully empty.

VIII

Martin is reading the proofs of *Outsider Iambics* at the kitchen table, trying to discern some common theme he can draw upon for his Introduction. So many people appeared to be outsiders that he was wondering whether there were any insiders at all. Dad comes in from the garden, where he has been complacently perusing crocuses. "What's that? Pomes?"

"Yeah – I gotta do an intro for them. It's harder than I thought it'd be."

"You'll be *fine*! You're just not used to this kind of thing! But you'll manage. You'll *more* than manage!" He sits down heavily at the table. His fingernails are dirty with clay. "Fi always said you was good with words – that you could do something with them! It's good to see other folks agreeing with her! Seriously, son, she'd be *proud* if she was here! *I'm* proud! About time a Hacklett *did* something, made his name at something!"

"Thanks, Dad – but you and Mum did something and all!"

"Dunno about that, son, but even if we did, it don't matter now! Used to think you might go on the River too, but just as well you didn't! That's all finished!" He nodded at the proofs. "Let's have a look at those."

He takes the thick wedge of paper and reads the first page. He reads it again. Then he opens the sheaf at random twice more and reads what he finds. He picks up the whole sheaf and riffles through it, as Martin watches his face. At last, he puts it down, and seems not to know what to say. "Well, son, all I can say is that they don't read like pomes to me! To me, they're not a patch on Kipling or Tennyson! Or have I just looked at the wrong ones?"

"Well, none of them are like Kipling or Tennyson! That's supposed to be the point – you know, new poems for a new century, a new kind of country. The idea is that they was insiders, and these poems are by *outsiders*."

Dad shakes his head. "To me, a pome's a pome, and it's either good or it ain't!"

"Between you and me, Dad, a lot of these ain't!"

They smile at each other, and Dad laughs. "I gotta hand it to you, Marty – writing about those in a way the writers won't mind will be a harder job than any *I* ever done! But if anyone can do it you can. Just mind how you go!" He exits crocus-wards, grinning at his boy's ingenuity.

Martin has just got back into the proofs – or as far into them as he can penetrate – when Mike clumps down the stairs and into the kitchen. He is looking more than usually podgy and dishevelled, and as he fills the kettle he farts. Martin marvels for perhaps the thousandth time that once he had thought his older brother the most admirable person in the world. Mike is about to turn on the radio when he realises that Martin has papers in front of him. "What's that? Pomes?"

"Yeah."

"Yours?"

"No – these are the ones I gotta write an article about."

"Let's have a look!"

"Don't fuck them up – they're all in order!"

But Mike handles them oddly gently, even if his face is a study in scorn. "*Outsider Iambics*? What's iambics?" Martin tells him. Mike flicks through the papers even more quickly than Dad had done. "Looks like bollocks to me, Marty! You gotta write something nice about *these*?"

Martin can't help smiling – and he can't remember the last time he smiled at his brother. "That's the idea!"

"Better you than me! And they asked you coz you're some kind of outsider too, yeah?"

"S'pose so."

Mike hands the poems back with a wry smile. "Funny, ain't it really – by having these published all you poetry plonkers become *insiders*, don't you?" He throws his teabag into the sink, and carries a mug of impossibly strong tea into the front room, from where almost immediately ensues the sound of some TV sport.

***

"Marty, when are you going to stop jumping?"

He squeezes her hand before replying. They are on a favourite walk – Greenwich to Charlton, past the Trinity Almshouses and the upturned pig of Greenwich Power Station, down along the river towards the O2 and eventually a pub. It is unseasonably mild for February, and someone is tooling around in midstream in a launch whose glistening black hull and growling engine are like a summation of speed. Martin watches the motorized whirligig moodily, envying the owner his potential for power. "It's not that easy now, is it, though?" he says at last. "I mean, I got a reputation now. It's *expected* of me! Do you think Seb or Hugo would be interested in me if I wasn't jumping? And you know the telly people want to shoot me in action. They're arranging everything already!"

"Well, I know you can't stop straight away ..."

But he had not quite finished defending himself. "Do you think Dad would be so proud if I stopped? Even Mike's proud of me! I think he really might try to get onto *Britain's Got Talent* now – just to outdo me! Besides, Katie, I *enjoy* it!"

"I don't care about Seb or that Hugo," she replies, feeling absurdly jealous of the journalist and his publisher friend, who seems to be always on the phone to Martin these days. "I do care about your Dad, though, and even Mike – a bit, anyway! But who I care about most is *you*! Every time you're up there I feel sick to my stomach, thinking this time he's gonna fall, this time he's gonna fall! I mean, I love you for doing it, but I hate you for doing it too, if you know wot I mean."

"But I know what I'm doing, Katie! I plan everything, I look at everything beforehand. I look at a wall and I *know* it – I know where I'll put this foot, then this one – where my hands'll go, if an overhang overhangs too much, if a plane's too steep or a gap's too wide. It'll sound stupid but I know a building as soon as I touch it! I kind of know if it'll be friendly! Does that sound stupid?"

"Yeah, Marty, it does! I know you're good and all that, but you can't foresee everything! What if a brick comes out, or a pipe breaks – or if you slip on ice or oil or something? And I don't think you're concentrating all the time now – you're always thinking about your book, and now the telly people. What if ..."

"I've had moments up there, I don't deny it, when I've nearly copped it. But that's *part* of it, see? If it wasn't dangerous there'd be no point, would there?"

"But *is* there a point, Marty? Or if there is a point, seems to me you've made it now. You've made your name, and thanks to that maybe there can be a future for you and me. Maybe there really *can* be a flat somewhere, or even a house – down in Bromley, maybe? Near the Common ..." She is wheedling, tickling his palm with a finger, although she knows she has lost for now.

"You *know* I want that, Katie – more than anything! But I can't give it up. Not yet. I need a few more months 'til the book comes out. So they can make the programme. That's all! Then we'll see! And we'll have a bit of money to play with."

He has a private agenda too, one she would laugh at. The black and white street atlas in which he traces his runs in yellow highlighter has become partly tricoloured, with large suburban swathes made neon, and whole pages bathed in bilious light except where there are parks, waterways or cemeteries, or no buildings worth leaping, or where there are but he cannot get to them. Seb and Hugo had been impressed when they saw it, and the hue had suggested to Hugo that Martin's book will be called *Jaundiced City*. But many pages are obstinately monochromatic, or have only little lurid stripes to mark border incursions. He has no wish to yellow the entire atlas, but some gaps irritate him, particularly those closest to home – two terraces in

Shooter's Hill, a tempting line of industrial units in Woolwich, a shopping centre in Catford. And then there's The Panopticon.

He has known Blackheath all his life, that high lung of the south city, airy and uplifting despite the A2 that crawls across it, seeming to offer prospects both into central London and deep into unconquered Kent. There are rugby goals and cricketers, and exhilarating expanses of grass. There is the haze over the river, visible even when the river itself is obscured by the worn walls of Greenwich Park. There is the Ranger's House, all old elegance and art. There is the hypodermic needle of a distant church, injecting the sky with intoxicants. And then there are all the fine houses, past which Dad had always towed his lads impatiently and with a strong hint of disapproval.

The worst offender in Dad's eyes, but the greatest attractant in Martin's, was always The Panopticon, a complex in old limestone whose dimensions, proportions and lawned setting had suggested to the impressionable boy what more of London might have looked like if only the right people had stayed in charge. And this Georgian geometry set has haunted him slightly ever since. He has even part-written a poem about it.

He is not to know that behind the Palladian facades are mazy dark and inconvenient apartments, inhabited by leaseholders uneasily aware they back onto notorious council housing – but even if he had known, it would not have made any difference. He has long yearned to climb and run it, to possess it that way if never in any other. The complex is subdivided into twelve equal-sized blocks arranged in a square, with ten foot wide gaps between each one, and no extensions or rooftop fans or fire escapes to ruin their superb symmetry. He knows few groups of buildings in London offer such a combination of handsomeness, height, size and evenness – it is like a racetrack in the air. Once he ran it while asleep, waking up part-disappointed that he had not really been, but more pleased that it was yet to come.

He has gone four times to try his luck, but there has always been some reason to postpone – once because there is a late-night party, once because much of it is stalky with scaffolding, and twice because police cars are parked close, as if the Bill are reminding themselves exactly what they are dedicated to defend. It has begun to look unlucky, but he will give it one last try. And then he can finish the poem. It will be one of his best runs, one of his best poems. The prospect enraptures, and he waxes brilliantly loquacious until Kate cannot help laughing, although she knows he is literally up to something.

They amble through the park at Charlton, where the aviary birds seem to be enjoying the mild weather – although neither likes seeing birds in cages – and then back past Charlton House to the church. Kate has always admired the red-brick church from the outside, whose tower always makes her think of *Vertigo* – and on an impulse they enter. They hush their voices automatically as they pass in, even though neither believes in anything. But there is something about the hushed hilltop interior, with its monuments to Woolwich military men and even an assassinated Prime Minister (they had not known there had even been one) that makes them feel vaguely that they have happened upon something significant – something just beyond understanding. They sit quietly near the back, speaking little, and almost in whispers. An elderly woman is putting flowers into vases, but then she disappears into the vestry.

"Marty?"

"Yeah?"

"What are you thinking?"

"I dunno, really – this place, all this history."

"Me too! Amazing, isn't it?"

"Yeah – yeah, it is. Dad'd *love* it! Wonder has he ever been here? We went to the house as kids, coz Dad wanted to see the mulberry trees. But I don't remember coming in here. Dad isn't religious, you see."

"He must have been here. These stone heads freak me out though!"

"I like them! They're strong, and they're real. They'll always be here, years after we've gone. Like the idea of that."

She shivered a bit. She was only wearing a thin coat, after all. "Well, *I* don't! They're all cold and dead. Give me the creeps!"

"Well don't look at them then!" He is gently mocking her.

She smiles back. "Wouldn't like to get married here with all them looking down on us!"

He puts his arm around her and pulls her to him, which she likes although it seems incongruous in a church. "Don't really think they'd mind, do you?" The flower woman comes back in, and they slide guiltily apart, although she is smiling at them brightly. They mumble hellos and leave as the light declines, walking quietly away down the hill.

***

Night. Stiff easterly. Scudding clouds. Celestial scimitar of moon. Car headlights poking across the heath. Trees leaning tiredly on the Park wall. A skinny fox trotting, destined for dustbins. Light spilling out of a door like blood from a wound, then staunched as it is swiftly shut against the cold, and things that creep. Now that there is suddenly some point to his poetry, Martin hears-sees music in everything. His eyes and ears seem newly sensitive, as if they have just been syringed. He hugs to himself the idea that any image he gathers may now find itself translated into print, gathered together in a proper book, his hedge against history.

The Panopticon looks quiet, cool and rational as he reaches its base and looks up. It is climbable, comprehensible. From up there, he should see so much of London, set out and contained like in his atlas. St. Paul's, The Shard, The Gherkin, The Cheesegrater, Lloyds, Bishopgate, Canary Wharf, Greenwich Hospital, the Queen's House, Charlton, Plumstead, Woolwich, Abbey Wood, Bexley, Eltham, Lewisham, Bromley, Forest Hill, Sydenham, Crystal Palace, Croydon, southwest to Richmond and far into Surrey, back into town again via the tower blocks of the Old Kent Road and the Elephant. And dividing and uniting London, the River with its tiny tributaries and tributaries of tributaries, bringing rain and dirt down from southern clay slopes to drain into the flood – the Kid Brook he just crossed, the Quaggy, Ravensbourne, Sluice, Peck, Effra, Neckinger and Falcon. He inhales with instantaneous excitement at the beauty and age of these names. It occurs to him that his *City* might be less jaundiced than Seb or Hugo would like.

He is touching the fantastical edifice finally. It trembles to his touch, as though in pleasure at meeting him – or are his hands shaking? He looks round one more time – all clear! There is a down pipe, which he tugs at – metal, sturdy. O.K. A sill there, another there. A stone armorial cartouche (martlets and wild men) – the stone is gleaming softly – finger-holds there, there, there. A parapet – easy, robust-looking. He will mount it like a marmoset. Clouds dash past in the same direction, sheep in front of some sky-shepherd.

He starts to ascend, and finds it absurdly easy. Almost disappointingly so, because the building is an ideal as well as an actual construction, and he wants each second to be remembered, and translatable into words that will cascade through all the Londons to come. Down pipe, sills, finger-holds, toeholds and parapet are all obedient, and no-one looks out to shout, and no police cars wander past. His muscles oil and mesh together – his back is to blackness, his face to the light.

He is up! – and safe, and everything is as still as anything can be in London. Here is The Panopticon he has promised himself. And he has not been over-optimistic, because he really can see into everything – and for the first time it looks back. The metropolis of eight-point-something million squats and throbs and winks slightly suggestively at Martin, almost welcoming him, as if acknowledging him as more-than-resident, as native, of this place for ages, owning it by right. And he takes it all in in a long inspiration, this city not yellow at all but white, while clouds flow and words crowd in from all sides and above. He is tracer of meanings as well as *traceur* – he is success, and Superhero.

The complex itself does not look complex from here, but as simple as kids' building blocks – and not well-made blocks, because he can see that some of the brickwork up here has been awry since the eighteenth century. And there is a huge and well-established puddle on the roof which is probably scummed and dirty by day – although tonight it is an oxidized mirror, throwing back quicksilver reflections of the Plough, the Pleiades, silver-rimmed clouds, and even a plane tracking across with winking lights. Capsules within capsules, worlds within worlds, upside-down universes inside universes, everything so cold and long ago. He watches the plane until it has passed out of the puddle and the sky is clear again, stars orbiting over what had once been countryside and might one day be again. That stellar conspectus, he decides, will form the central motif of his Panopticon Canto. ("We are all in the gutter, but...") He will remember it for the rest of his life.

He looks up at last from the trembling water. Ten minutes have somehow passed; he has never spent so long on a roof. It is too long, because movement defines him. He cannot under any circumstances get caught, be taken down. He must move, do what he came to do, see what he came to see, get down, write it down, move on. It is a simple square he needs to circle, and he has anticipated every angle. He just needs to put one leg in front of the other over and over again, get into the rhythm of left-right-left-right recurring more and more rapidly, sing the song of heart and lung, feel the ecstasy of empty as he sails across gulfs, and of safe as he lands on each far side.

With a last all-encompassing look, and a preparatory breath, he powers up like the engine he has always been, and begins to piston. Across the first roof he starts to streak – ball-in-socket, sinew-thew, ball-in-socket, sinew-thew, blood like jet fuel, gathering speed, gaining grace as he goes, smiling oh *what* a run! – feet ever faster and further apart as the background blurs and for a second he sees himself from outside, considers how small and neat a thing he is, how very fast and furious, a blond berserker leading with his left across the high huge vacancy of life...

...but falling short.

Printed in Great Britain
by Amazon